Nobody Knows

How Much

I Love You

By: Jamie K Coyne

Disclaimer

This is a work of fiction. Names, characters, places, events, and incidents are either the products of the author's imagination or used in a fictitious manner. Any resemblance to actual persons, living or dead, or actual events is purely coincidental.

Chapter 1

Justin and I had been best friends ever since I can remember. I think it was because both of our mums were in the hospital with us at the same time. They became friends, and then, once we were born, we spent so much time together, we automatically became friends. As you probably guessed, Justin and I have very close birthdays; however, he is 2 days older than me. And he never lets me forget it. On the rare occasions we have arguments, especially when we were kids, he always plays the I-know-best-because-I'm-older-than-you card. It used to wind me up, but now I just ignore it.

When we were Juniors in high school, I finally got up the guts to tell Justin that I was gay. It was weird, I wasn't scared to tell my family or any of my friends, but I was freaking terrified of Justin's response. And not because he'd previously expressed any hatred towards gay people. Simply because he was the most important person in my life, and if he didn't approve of my lifestyle, then it would kill me. However, Justin's very laid back response was, "whatever floats your boat." At that point, I had thrown myself into his arms and hugged him tightly, never wanting to let him go. Justin had simply burst out laughing and held me back. This wasn't anything new to him – we'd always had this sort of relationship; the touchy, feely type. And I was glad that that didn't have to change because Justin was awkward hugging me because I was gay.

By the time I worked up the guts to tell Justin the truth, I'd known I was gay for several years. Of course, I'd always wondered...I'd never been especially attracted to girls. But, when I was fourteen and Justin and I went to the beach with my parents, and I found myself getting embarrassingly aroused when I saw Justin in his swimming trunks, I could no longer deny it. I knew I was gay.

I then started the whole dating thing, which I hadn't tried up until then. Justin, who by that time had had several girlfriends, kept trying to set me up, but I wasn't comfortable going out with random guys. I wanted something more, I wanted someone special. However, to make Justin happy – because he thought I was upset that I was single – I went out on a couple of dates. But nothing worked. They were all nice guys. Just not right for me.

Only about a year later, halfway through our senior year, I came to the next realization. This one probably bigger and more life-altering than the first.

I was in love with my best friend. My *best friend* who was undoubtedly **straight.**

Chapter 2

Chris had been my best friend since the second I was born. I knew this without a shadow of a doubt. How could we be such good friends now and not have been best friends the second we met? And just because we were weeks old doesn't mean we couldn't have been friends. I know, I just *know*, that we were always best friends. And we always will be.

I remember the time, in junior year, when Chris had told me his secret. I had wanted to say something more important, I'd planned to say something more important when he finally told me, but when the moment came, I completely forgot to act like I didn't already know and just shrugged off his comment. I'd always known he was gay... Well, not *always*, but the second he knew, I knew. He was just too easy to read. Especially after knowing him for 17 years. No one else cared he was gay. There was the occasional jock at school who bullied him, but he didn't care. He didn't let it bother him, and I was incredibly proud of him for that.

Over the last year, I have been constantly setting him up and trying to get him on dates. I know how great it feels when I have a girlfriend, so all I want is for him to have that with someone as well. But whenever he does get a boyfriend, they never last more than a month. I was starting to think he was just insanely fussy when he stopped dating altogether.

And it frustrated me more than I possibly imagined when I couldn't figure out why he'd stopped dating. And he wouldn't tell me, which hurt. Our whole lives we'd shared everything, told each other everything. He was the person I came running to when I had my first kiss with Stacy when I had been 13. I was so excited I just *had* to tell him. I knew he would be happy for me, and he was. So, in the past, Chris and I had shared all our thoughts, not leaving anything unsaid to each other. Which was why it hurt impossibly much when I realized he was keeping something from me. He wasn't telling me why he was upset. He wasn't telling me why he'd suddenly stopped dating.

I know it's childish...but for that reason alone, I decided not to tell Chris my secret. He didn't want to share with me, I wasn't going to share with him.

Chapter 3

-Chris-

During our senior year, Justin and I did what most teenagers do. We partied. It was at these parties that Justin usually picked up his girlfriends, who then lasted a short period of time. Justin only really wanted a girlfriend for one reason. And while I didn't agree with that at all, I'd given up on trying to convince Justin to strive for a more meaningful relationship with a girl. All Justin was interested in were one night stands.

I quickly grew tired of the constant parties, but it was where Justin thrived, so I went along just to spend time with him. Not that I didn't spend all day with him anyway. But I just didn't want to be apart from him. And besides, if forced, I could have fun at a party. I just ignored most of the people around me and focused on the beautiful boy who flirted his way around the room, narrowing down his options until he found the one he wanted. Justin's approach to getting a girl was, to be honest, disgusting, but he'd perfected it so much over the last few years that it worked like a charm.

Justin often had several girls hanging around him. Begging him to dance with them, desperate for him to take them home. I couldn't help the grimace that came over my face every time Justin and I left a party, one lucky, drunk girl hanging off his arm. I hated him for the way he treated his girls. But I knew that wasn't him. Not really. This was just a blip, a faze he was going through that I knew he would come out of. At parties, Justin wasn't the boy I loved. He was a pig.

Except tonight. Tonight he was...different. He just had no enthusiasm. By this time of night, he would be dancing with 2 or more girls...but he wasn't. I frowned as I watched him from across the room. I'd just gotten myself a drink – coke because I was driving – and when I turned to find Justin amongst the people on the dance floor, I couldn't see him. And it worried me. But it didn't worry me as much as his face did. He looked upset. He looked lonely. He looked...confused.

I bit my lip before slowly going over to him, my eyes searching his face constantly, trying to find a clue as to why he was so upset. I sat next to him and he didn't react. I frowned more, even more worried. He was usually so vibrant at parties, so full of life... But now...he was just dead. "Justin, what's wrong?" I asked over the music.

"There's no one here," he replied and I frowned, confused.

"What are you talking about?" I asked him. "There are tons of people here."

"Not that I want," he said and realisation hit me and I moved away from him slightly. There was no one here who he wanted to sleep with. I shook my head slightly, but then did my duty as best friend and tried to cheer him up.

"What about her?" I asked, looking at a blonde across the room, whose eyes kept moving to Justin.

"No..." Justin sighed and I looked back at him and frowned. Had he even looked?

"Okay then, what about her?" I asked, indicating with my hand in a general direction where I guessed a girl would be standing.

"No," Justin replied again, without lifting his gaze from the floor.

"J, what's wrong?" I asked again, knowing that it wasn't the lack of girls that was upsetting him.

"Nothing," he said, suddenly standing up. "I'm gonna get a drink." He then walked away and I knew then that he was going to drink himself into oblivion tonight. When he was in a good mood, with plenty of girls to choose from, he got drunk. So when he was upset, he would drink even more.

I shook my head again as I stood up and went to follow him. But people kept getting in my way and I lost track of him. I wanted to try to keep an eye on him, knowing that it would be my toilet that he would be throwing up into later, but I couldn't find him anywhere. I sighed and continued walking round and round the house, trying hopelessly to find Justin.

Chapter 4

-Justin-

I don't know why I was upset tonight. More than any other night... Maybe I was just sick of acting "straight". Maybe I was just sick of the girls. I wanted to tell Chris the truth, but after keeping it a secret for nearly a year, I just couldn't. I didn't know how he would react, for one thing. I didn't know if he'd hate me for not telling him. After all, he'd told me he was gay, so I should have the guts to do the same thing... But I was scared of everyone else as well. I was comfortable acting straight for now. I was used to it and people accepted me. But that's not all I want to tell him. I want to tell him how I feel about him, that I love him as much more than a friend, more than a best friend. But I can't. It's seriously unlikely that he'll reciprocate, and there's no chance in hell that I'm going to ruin our friendship. If I lose Chris I don't know what I'd do.

Instead, I spent all night avoiding Chris. Every time I saw him approaching me, I quickly ducked and ran out of the room. I wanted to talk to him, just simply spend time with him, but I couldn't. Not without wanting more. I went through to the kitchen and drank a shot of something. I didn't know what it was, but it burnt my throat as I swallowed. I didn't want to get drunk tonight – I just wasn't in the mood. But I didn't want Chris to know that. I didn't want him to know I was upset, so I had to pretend to be okay. Therefore, I had to drink. I picked up another shot and downed that one as well. I coughed slightly and then walked away from the kitchen. I didn't want anymore. I wanted to stay in control.

I staggered out of the room, already playing my role, and found Chris. "Can we go?" I asked him, slinging my arm around his shoulders. I knew he'd smelt the alcohol on my breath because I saw him scowl and turn away from me.

"Sure," he said and we started walking towards the door. I put extra weight on Chris and his supporting arm around me tightened. I felt my heart speed up considerably and I moved slightly closer to Chris. And he didn't seem to mind. He just held me even closer. I smiled softly and continued to stumble to his car. "How much did you drink...?" Chris mumbled as I tripped over my own feet.

"I had a lot to drink," I grinned and Chris rolled his eyes.

"Yeah, I know," he said. I didn't realize how tenderly he treated me when I was drunk... He's always the one who looks after me when I drink too much...I just couldn't remember how he acted. When we reached his car, he unlocked the doors and then gently placed me in the passenger seat.

"Okay?" he asked as I leant heavily against the seat. I nodded and Chris smiled softly and brushed my hair out of my face. I looked up at him, my heart skipping a beat, but he was already moving away and shutting the door. I looked down again and curled up in my chair, leaning my head on the window. Chris really was the best friend a guy could ever ask for. He was perfect. I turned to look at him and watched him driving. I bit my lip before speaking.

"You're perfect, Chrissy," I slurred, grinning at him. He snorted and then cracked a grin at me.

"And you're drunk," he said and I shrugged. Apparently me saying that to him was nothing new. I wondered briefly what else I'd said to him in my drunken states, but I didn't really care.

We got back to his house about 15 minutes later. I waited for Chris to get out of the car and open my door, before awkwardly climbing out of the car. I grabbed Chris' hand, once it was offered, to pull myself up. I then leant against him, leaning my head on his shoulder. "I don't feel so good, Chrissy," I mumbled and Chris laughed.

"Shocking," he said sarcastically. "Come on. Let's get you in bed." I smiled to myself but he didn't see. We then started walking to his front door. He pulled his keys out of his pocket and unlocked the door. I frowned slightly. His parents always left the door unlocked when Chris was out, so it was easy for him to get in, or if he lost his keys he wasn't locked out. So I guessed his parents were out for the night. I bit my lip as an idea formed in my head. I was "drunk" so I couldn't be held accountable for my actions...not really.

Chris led me up to his room and placed me on his bed before turning away. I fell back and lay on my back. "Chrissy," I sighed, staring up at the ceiling. "There weren't any girls tonight..."

"I know, you told me already," he replied patiently.

"But I need someone...I *need* it," I said desperately. I watched as Chris turned around and looked at me. He was frowning, confused. I sat up and then climbed off the bed and walked over to him. "I need it," I repeated as I pressed my body against his. I heard his shocked gasp and I felt his body stiffen.

"Jus...what are you doing?" he asked. I bit the inside of my lip as I debated whether to continue. But I decided to hell with it. If it all went horribly wrong, I had the excuse that I was so drunk I didn't know what I was doing.

"Chrissy...I need...*it*," I said, pressing myself further against Chris. Chris took a step backwards and I followed until he was pressed against the wall and I was pressing against his front. I felt something interesting pressing against my hip but I decided to ignore it...for now. "I need sex. Please," I begged. I saw Chris' eyes widen slightly but I then pressed my lips against his and his face seemed to instantly relax. His eyes closed and mine quickly followed. He moaned softly in his throat and I grasped his body tightly in my arms.

"Oh, God," he whispered as my lips left his and kissed over his neck.

"Justin...you have to stop..."

Even as he said it I could feel his resistance breaking. I just stubbornly shook my head and then pulled his shirt over his head. I gazed at his beautiful chest. Of course, I had seen it many times before, but this seemed different...much more intimate due to the knowledge of what was about to come. I lowered my head and kissed and licked my way across his chest and I heard his gasps and moans and couldn't help but grin. I moved my hands to his belt but he finally pushed me away. I looked up into his eyes but I didn't see what I was expecting. His eyes were no longer hesitant or unsure. His eyes were full of lust and desire. That look alone almost had me coming in my pants. I swallowed hard and he reached out and pulled my shirt off me. I raised my eyes and met his gaze. We looked into each other's eyes for what felt like an eternity but then I grabbed his shoulders and practically threw him onto his bed. I heard his gasp but then I was lying over him and kissing him deeply. Our bare chests rubbed together, causing both of us to moan into the kiss. I suddenly felt Chris' hands at my hips and then my jeans were being quickly forced off of me. I hurried to do the same to him, pulling his boxers off at the same time. I moaned as I saw his cock spring free. "Fuck..." I heard Chris moan. His hands quickly went to my boxers and he pushed them down. I hissed in a breath as the cool air hit my cock, and then again as Chris' hand wrapped around me.

"Jesus..." I moaned and I leant down and rested my head on his shoulder.

"I need...I need to-"

"I know," Chris whispered. It surprised me for a second, that his voice was back to tenderness. "Fuck me," he said and I groaned. I knew I should ask him for a condom but I wanted to feel him. Besides, I knew I didn't have anything, and I trusted Chris. Additionally, I knew he hadn't slept with anyone yet.

I suddenly froze. This was his first time. That thought alone was almost enough to make me want to stop. This isn't how one would imagine your first time, with your drunk best friend. I didn't want to take that away from him, either. I was about to pull away, but Chris clung to me. I looked down at him and saw he wanted, needed, this just as much as I did. I knew this was going to hurt him. I lined myself up to his entrance. I kissed him passionately as I pushed in slowly. My kiss didn't prevent him from screaming, however. And the noise went straight to my heart. I stopped immediately, waiting for some sign that he was okay. Then I felt him move his hips up towards mine and I knew he was ready for more. I pushed in again, slowly so slowly. I could feel him breathing heavily under me and I realized how proud I was of him. This couldn't be comfortable for him. Finally, I was in all the way and I stayed still, waiting. "Move!" Chris commanded and I smirked slightly and then pulled backwards and then thrust back inside him.

"So...tight," I gasped. Chris lifted his hips in time with my thrusts, deepening my thrusts. He was constantly moaning underneath me and the sight turned me on even more. "Fuck..." I moved my hand to his cock between us and started trying to bring him off in time with myself. I already knew neither of us was going to last very long.
"Fuck, Justin," Chris gasped and it was then that I realised how great it

sounded to hear him moan my name.

I suddenly realized what I was doing. I was having sex with my best friend...I was *making love* to my best friend. A boy. I was sleeping with a boy, who was going to remember this tomorrow. I could pretend I didn't remember, but he would. He would know that I am gay...or at least...he could guess. I was just going to have to act extra hard to act straight to hide it.

Only minutes later, I felt myself ready to come, and I could tell by Chris writhing beneath me, that he was too. I pumped his cock hard and felt him clench around me tightly. I moaned and then came; Chris' name a whisper on my lips.

Chapter 5

-Chris-

Justin had rolled off me and hugged me to his side immediately. My heart was still pounding in my chest half an hour, by which time Justin had fallen asleep. I can't believe I let that happen. What was going to happen tomorrow? He wouldn't remember...he'd been completely hammered. But what if he did? He wasn't gay...he'll be disgusted with himself if he found out what happened. He'll be disgusted with me if he found out. And I couldn't stand that.

I made the most of lying in Justin's arms, but then I slid out of bed. I pulled on a pair of boxers and then left the room. I went to the guest room and climbed into bed in there. It was cold and empty. It was lacking Justin. I needed his arms back around me, holding me as though he wanted me, as though he loved me.

Tears rolled down my cheeks as I thought about how huge of a mistake I had just made. If Justin remembers tomorrow, or if he suddenly remembers in a few weeks or months, our relationship will be ruined. And if he doesn't remember, I will. I'll have to be around him as though nothing happened. I'll have to pretend that he didn't just take my virginity and I'd never experienced anything quite as mind-blowing as that. Justin had been everything I wanted and more.

I cried myself to sleep that night.

When I woke up the memories instantly came flooding back to me. It had been the best, and the worst, night of my life and I couldn't figure out how I really felt about it. I mean, of course I was happy that Justin had been my first...but I just wish it was because he wanted me and not just because he wanted a fuck.

I rolled out of bed and went to the bathroom and did my usual routine. I then went to my room to wake up Justin, but he wasn't there. I frowned slightly and pulled on a t-shirt quickly. I heard the sound of clanging from the kitchen and went downstairs and headed towards the noise. My stomach was filled with butterflies. What was going to happen once I walked into the room? Would he remember? My brain was telling me no, he wouldn't remember, he was drunk. But, in a strange way, my heart was praying that he did remember and he was okay with it.

I walked into the kitchen and immediately tensed when I saw him standing the other side of the room dressed in nothing but boxers. I bit my lip before stepping further into the room and making my presence known. Justin turned around and smiled at me. I smiled back sadly. Just from the smile I knew he didn't remember. From that smile I knew he thought last night never happened. I swallowed hard and then went and sat down. I winced slightly as I put weight on my bruised behind. I heard Justin snort and I looked up to see him smirking. "Fun night last night?" he asked and I froze. Could I have read him wrongly? Did he remember? "Do you like the guy?" he asked as he sat down opposite me. I looked away from him. He wouldn't remember; he'd had too much to drink. "It was a one night stand," I said. I couldn't stand being in the same room as him any longer so I stood up again from the chair and left the room – managing not to limp. I knew Justin would want to ask more questions, for example, 'since when do you have one night stands?' or 'you didn't answer my question...' And I wasn't going to stick around and talk to him about having sex with him when he didn't remember.

I went upstairs and had a long, hot shower, relaxing my body. The entire time I was in the shower, I was hoping that by the time I got back downstairs, Justin would be gone.

Chapter 6

-Justin-

I looked down as I watched Chris walk out of the room. I hadn't meant to hurt him, I hadn't meant to cause him pain – not emotionally. But that seems to be all I do recently. And now I had to pretend like the best night of my life never happened. I had to act as though I was straight... But...I was sort of glad of the fact that I had the alcohol to hide behind. Because I wasn't ready to come out. I wasn't ready for everyone to know about me yet. I guess telling Chris would be okay – I knew he wouldn't tell anyone – but that would mean admitting that I had been sober and I had tricked him last night. And I didn't want to hurt him any more than I already had.

So, instead of running away which is what my instincts were telling me to do, I made myself a coffee and toast and then moved into the living room and watched television as I waited for Chris to come back down. I didn't know what he was doing, I didn't know if he was freaking out... I wanted to go and see if he was okay, but if I was to play my part, I had to act as though I had no reason to assume he was upset.

About an hour later, Chris came staggering through the door, rubbing his wet hair in a towel. He froze when he saw me. Regret slammed into me. He was awkward being around me. "You're still here?" he asked and my heart twisted.

"Yeah, why wouldn't I be?" I asked, pretending that I didn't know.

"Um...no reason..." he replied and I smiled slightly and nodded, turning back to the television. I realized that Chris was still standing in the doorway, not knowing what to do.

"You okay?" I asked and he nodded, not meeting my eyes. He came and sat on the sofa next to me. It was clear to me that he was forcing himself to be relaxed and normal. I know that I would usually ask him what was wrong, pester him into telling me, but I didn't want to today because I felt too guilty to ask him to talk about something he clearly is uncomfortable with. God, I shouldn't have done that last night...I just thought that he'd want me as much as I wanted him.

We sat watching television for about another hour. Normally, if we watched tv together, Chris would end up curling against my side and leaning his head on my shoulder. But he didn't this time and I missed it desperately. I wanted to wrap my arms around him, but I didn't normally do that until he leaned against me first. And if this was going to work, I had to be normal. I had to do what Chris would expect. So we sat there on the sofa, our bodies inches apart, yet the distance between us had never felt bigger.

I forced myself to stay with Chris until 6 p.m. when I said I had to get home. I didn't have to and I think he knew that, but he nodded anyway. "I'll see you tomorrow at school," I smiled as we walked to the door. "Pick me up as normal?" I don't know why I'd felt I had to ask that, but I needed to hear the answer.

"Yeah, sure," Chris smiled at me. I smiled back relieved. I leaned forward and hugged him tightly, quickly, inhaling his sweet smell. I felt Chris tensed slightly but I pretended not to notice it. I smiled at him again as I pulled away and started walking home.

It wasn't a long walk, but I was glad for the time alone. It gave me more time to think about my actions...more time to regret how I acted. What I wouldn't give to go back in time and stop myself. Not to save myself any heartache, because I completely deserve it for how I acted, but to save Chris. He doesn't deserve feeling uncomfortable around me because of my idiocy. How could I make things go back to how they were before? How could I make Chris treat me in the way he used to? How could I fix what was left of our friendship?

Chapter 7

-Chris-

I hated to admit that I was relieved once Justin left. Never before had I felt that way, but I hated being awkward around him so much that I'd rather simply not be around him. I wish I could go back and be stronger, be able to say no, but I couldn't. And now I had to suffer the consequences of my weak self-control. I went back up to my room and looked at my bed. The sheets were ruffled, pulled away from the mattress; the pillows still had a slight indent from where Justin had lain. My eyes scanned back over the bed, taking in the stains, and I sighed. I stripped the bed, leaving my mattress bare and then went to put all the linens in the wash.

I then went into the kitchen and made myself a bowl of pasta. I glanced at the clock as I stirred the cooking pasta and saw it was 6.45. My parents had said they would be home at around 8, which meant they wouldn't be back until 8.30 at the earliest. I didn't want to talk to them, I didn't want to talk to anyone, but 8.30 was too early to pull off being asleep. I sat in the living room eating slowly and watching television. Nothing much was on, but I forced myself to watch it to keep my mind away from Justin.

By 9 o'clock, my parents still weren't home but I decided to go up to bed anyway. I was still exhausted from the night before and was dying for a good night's sleep. I then remembered that I hadn't remade my bed and sighed. I pulled clean sheets out of the cupboard and then set about making my bed. I hated to make my bed because it was a double bed and it was big. I put one corner of the sheet on the mattress, moved to the next corner and the first would spring off. Justin usually helped me whenever my mum nagged me to change my bed...but I couldn't ask him now. Simply because it would be too awkward.

After managing to successfully make the bed, I tiredly took my clothes off and stuffed them in my closet, telling myself I would put them away properly tomorrow. Dressed only in my boxers I climbed into bed, lay back and sighed. I closed my eyes and started to relax. But then images of last night came into my head and I forced my eyes open. Fuck, I had to get Justin out of my head! I forced myself to think about school, about some random homework assignments. I managed to make myself so bored thinking about that subject that before I knew it, I was dead to the world.

When I next opened my eyes, sunlight was streaming in through my windows. I sighed as I realized I hadn't shut the curtains and it was only 5.30. I moaned and fell back into my pillows, burying my face under my duvet. I closed my eyes and miraculously managed to fall asleep for another 2 hours.

When my alarm went off at 7.30, waking me up for school, I moaned again. I was going to see Justin in about half an hour... I went to my closet and opened the doors, yesterday's clothes falling out onto my feet. I just ignored them and searched for something to wear. I pulled out a pair of black skinny jeans and an All-Time Low t-shirt. I glanced outside and then quickly grabbed a green zip-up hoodie. I went downstairs and into the kitchen. My parents weren't around, but their bedroom door had been shut, so I guessed they were still asleep. I wondered what time they got home, but the shrugged. As long as they didn't wake me up I didn't care. I quickly made myself some toast and sat eating it at the kitchen table. I glanced at the clock and saw it was 5 minutes to 8. I sighed, I was going to be late picking Justin up. I quickly grabbed my bag while yanking on my shoes. I found my keys and then quickly left the house and headed to my car.

Ten minutes later, I was pulling up outside of Justin's house. I noticed him looking through the window and smiled in relief when he saw me pull up. When he disappeared from sight I wondered why he was relieved I was here...maybe it was just because I was a bit late. Seconds later, Justin's front door opened and he appeared, wearing dark blue skinny jeans, a white t-shirt, and a red hoodie. I took my eyes away from him as he walked towards me. I couldn't let my eyes stay on him for too long. "Hey," he smiled as he opened the passenger door. I turned to him and smiled. "Morning, you okay?" I asked as he shut the door. He nodded and I smiled slightly before starting the car and continuing the drive to school.

We didn't arrive late, we were right on time. Once I had parked, Justin and I both jumped out of the car and headed to our classroom. "Hey guys!" Justin and I both turned to see Zoe and Jake coming towards us. We both smiled in response.

"Hey, you alright?" Justin asked them and they both nodded. Justin and I had been friends with the couple since we'd started high school. We had a fairly large group of friends, but us four were the closet. Of course, no one is closer than Justin and I, but we both considered Zoe and Jake good friends.

After our first class I went to the bathroom, telling Justin I would meet him in English next period. He just nods. He's been acting weird since we got to school, but I hadn't commented. I didn't want him to say anything about Saturday night. So I went to the bathroom, did my business, and was about to head to my next class when I remembered I didn't have my file. I sighed before heading to my locker.

I froze, my heart in my throat, as my locker came into sight. Justin was by it. But he wasn't alone. He was standing there, pressing a random girl against the metal and practically eating her face off. I think I actually felt my heartbreak.

Chapter 8

I stood, unsure of what I was feeling as I watched Katie run away. "Who was that?" I turned to see Chris standing behind me. My heart twisted as I saw the pain he was trying hard to hide.

"Katie," I said, glad I'd overheard one of her friends call her. Otherwise, I'd have no idea what the hell her name was. "I just asked her out."

"And you're making out already?" he asked angrily. I frowned slightly.

"What's your problem?" I asked him and he instantly backed off. I saw his face basically crumple before he shook his head and started walking away. The only reason I'd asked her out was to make sure things carried on as 'normal'. I frequently asked girls out...it was fair that I didn't usually go straight to making out with them...but I couldn't help but want to prove that inside I was still me. "Fuck," I muttered as I followed after him, going to English.

Chris wasn't in the room and I frowned, worried. I wanted to go and look for him, to make sure he was alright, but Mrs. Smith had already seen me so I couldn't leave the room. I slowly, regretfully, made my way over to my desk, half of which should occupy Chris. It felt weird not having Chris next to me. He was always here. I couldn't remember a time when he wasn't around and I didn't know why. It's fair to say that I didn't learn a thing all lesson because my head was on Chris, wondering where he was and if he was okay.

After English it was lunch and I headed to the cafeteria. Chris wasn't there either. I frowned but went and got my lunch anyway and sat at a table with Zoe, Jake, and several other friends. "Where's Chris?" Zoe asked me.

"I don't know..." I said and realized that was the first time I'd ever said
that. Zoe frowned slightly, probably shocked at the fact that I didn't know
where Chris was. I poked at my food for a while but couldn't eat anything.
"I'm going to go look for him." Zoe smiled and nodded. I stood up and
quickly walked out of the loud room. Something wasn't right. Sure, I'd
understand not coming to English...I mean, I know I'd hurt him, but he
wouldn't not come to lunch. He'd know that I would come looking for
him at lunch when I couldn't during a lesson. I went to the nearest
bathroom first, the one that he would have gone to if he had come here to
hide. "Chris?" I called out and heard a small gasp. I frowned slightly and
walked to the end of the bathroom. I looked around the corner and my
breath left my lungs as tears gathered in my eyes.

Chris was curled in a corner. His eyes were red, clearly he'd been crying,
but that wasn't my top concern. His lip was split, bleeding down his chin.
His eye already had a black bruise forming around it. And just the way his
clothes were rumbled suggested that he had bruises all over his body.
"What happened, Chris?" I asked softly as I sat on the cold tiles next to
him. I saw him move away from me slightly and I hated it. I bit my lip
before reaching out and pulling him against me. No matter what was going
on between us, I wasn't going to let him suffer alone. I felt him struggle for
a second, but soon he relaxed against me. He turned his head and buried
his head in my shoulder. His hands clutched at my shirt as he held
himself tighter to me. "Chris, talk to me, please," I whispered as I stroked
his hair softly.

"H-He...because...I'm g-gay," he whispered. His voice was so weak, so
tired, and my heart cried for him.

"I'm so sorry," I whispered, wrapping my arms tighter around him. I had
to really control myself. I wanted to kiss him to make it better. I even had

to put in a conscious effort not to call him 'baby' at the end of each sentence...

After a short while I pulled away slightly. I felt Chris cling to me tighter before quickly pulling away when he realized what he'd done. "You should go to the nurse," I told him and he shook his head.

"I'm okay," he said. I stood up and then held my hands out for him to help him up. He smiled slightly and put his hands in mine. I then pulled him up, but he cried out in pair and sank back to the floor, clutching his ribs.

"What did he do?" I asked desperately, crouching in front of him.

"Kicked..." he gasped out and I bit my lip.

"Was it Jared?" I asked. Chris glanced up at me before lowering his head again and nodding. "Fuck." I knew what Jared was like. Anything he could do to hurt a gay person was satisfying for him. People like him were part of the reason I was scared to come out. "Do you think you can walk?" I asked him. He took a deep breath, wincing slightly and then nodded. "Sure?" I asked, not wanting him to hurt himself further.

"Just help me up," he said. I moved next to him, putting his arm over my shoulders. I wrapped my arm around his middle and pulled him up slowly and gently.

"Okay?" I asked him. I looked at him and saw his eyes were scrunched shut. He nodded and I knew he was lying. "I'm taking you to the nurse." When Chris didn't argue I knew I'd made the right decision and that Chris knew it.

As we walked through the corridors towards the nurse's room, neither of us said anything. I was about to start talking when someone called my name. I was slightly relieved that I had been saved from talking, but then slightly angry for the same reason. Chris and I both turned and we saw Katie approaching. I felt Chris tense in my arms slightly. Katie walked straight up to me and kissed me. I wanted to pull away but I knew I shouldn't. I needed her. "Do you want to go for a walk?" she asked. "Um," I said. I glanced at Chris and then away. Is this what I'd normally do? I didn't even know. My head and my heart were screaming at me to stay with Chris, but some voice in my head was telling me that I had to prove to Chris that I was still me. I turned to Chris and I knew from the look in his eyes that he already knew what was coming. "You okay, right? You can get to the nurse from here?" I asked, disgusted at the words coming out of my mouth. Chris didn't respond but I slid out from under his arm anyway. Katie linked her arm with mine and we started walking away.

It was then that I realized I would never, *ever*, put someone else, especially some random girl, in front of Chris. This wasn't normal behavior for me. *Fuck*

Chapter 9

-Chris-

I stood staring, my mouth slightly open in shock, as I watched Justin walk off. I couldn't believe he'd left me! How could he just leave me when I could barely walk? I felt tears prickling in the corners of my eyes and I bit my lip hard to stop myself from crying. "Chris? What the fuck happened to you? Justin said he was coming to find you..." I turned around and saw Zoe approaching. When she met my eyes, her eyes widened and she hurried towards me. As soon as she got next to me I leant against her, needing to take some weight off my ribs. "What happened?" she asked again. "Where's Justin?" I nodded in the direction that Justin had walked, where he was still in sight with Katie hanging off him. Zoe turned and looked and gasped. "Bastard," she said and I nodded. But no matter what he did, I couldn't help but love him. I knew he wasn't intentionally hurting me, this was just who he was. He put his girlfriends in front of his friends... I frowned slightly. He didn't usually do that...maybe this was a new Justin...

"Just..help me get to the nurse," I managed to say. She nodded and we started walking towards the nurse's office. We didn't say anything as we walked, but I could tell that Zoe wanted to ask.

We walked through the door and Nurse Spencer stood quickly.

"Chris...what happened this time?" she asked me. I didn't reply, my lip was too swollen to waste the effort on speaking pointless sentences. She knew what happened; it was the same thing that always happened. She just shook her head and came over to me. She didn't ask who had done it, because she knew I wouldn't tell. She brought a cool cloth up to my lip and dabbed at the bleeding cut. I winced slightly.

"My ribs..." I said softly as I sat on a chair tenderly.

"Lean back for me," she said and I did, biting my lip as I did so. She lifted my shirt and as I glanced down I already saw dark bruises forming. Nurse Spencer placed two fingers gently on my sides to feel my ribs. She did this for a while and then moved to the other side. "You're lucky, none are broken, just severely bruised," she said and I nodded, pulling my shirt back down. "Chris-"

"No," I said. "I'm not saying anything to anyone."

"But this is serious," she said desperately and I shook my head.

"Chris-" Zoe said and I stood up, ignoring the pain.

"No," I said again and walked out of the room. Neither Zoe nor Nurse Spencer followed me. I walked for a few minutes and then gave up and leant against the wall nearest me.

I heard a bell go, signalling start of lessons but I didn't move. I wasn't going to be able to get to my class. I sank down to the floor as tears rolled down my cheeks. Why was my life so fucked up? I leant my head back against the wall and pulled my phone out of my pocket. I dialled Justin's number and waited for him to answer. Even though he was in class, I hoped he would answer. "Chris?" he asked softly, trying to hide the fact that he was on the phone.

"Justin..." I cried. "P-Please can you t-take me...home?"

"Mr Thompson, I have to go to the bathroom," I heard Justin say. I didn't hear a response, however, before I heard the classroom door open and quickly shut. "Where are you?" he asked me.

"Just round the corner from the nurse's office," I said quietly. I heard Justin's heavy breathing, suggesting he was running. I didn't let the fact that he was so concerned get to me. So what if he was showing how much he cared now? He'd left me before.

Heavy footfalls from my right drew my attention and I turned to see Justin running towards me. He dropped down to the floor next to me and pulled me into his chest. I felt him shaking slightly and I buried my head in his shoulder. I didn't want to cry, but couldn't help but have more tears run down my cheek. I eventually pulled back. I noted that Justin's eyes were slightly red but I didn't comment. "Chris, I-" he started but I cut him off.

"Just take me home, please," I said pulling away from him. He frowned slightly but nodded. He stood and then bent down and pulled me up, quickly but smoothly. I winced slightly and leant into him, needing him to help me but wishing I didn't.

"I'm sorry," he whispered. I didn't know if he meant for me to hear because he'd said it so quietly so I didn't reply. I wasn't sure what he was apologising for...whether it was because he'd hurt me when he pulled me up, or because he'd broken my heart when he chose Katie over me.

Chapter 10

Chris didn't reply when I apologized, but I didn't blame him for not forgiving me. I know I'd hurt him too much. I didn't understand how I could possibly hurt my best friend so much in such a short period of time. But I'd managed. We walked slowly to Chris' car and he passed me his keys. I could drive, but I didn't have a car, which is why Chris had to drive me everywhere...not that he ever complained. I took his keys but first I helped him into the car, making sure he was comfortable before shutting the door. As I walked around the car I watched Chris. He lowered his head and shook it slightly and I frowned. I wanted to know what he was thinking, but I was scared to ask.

I got into the car and glanced over at him again before I started the engine. He was looking out the window, but not at anything in particular. I hated that he was looking in the opposite direction because he was scared to look at me. I bit my lip and got over myself. I reached over and took his hand in mine. Chris' head snapped around and he stared at me wide-eyed. "You sure you're okay?" I asked him while squeezing his hand. When I saw his eyes soften and a small smile tug at the corners of his lips I knew I'd done the right thing. This was how I normally acted.
"Yeah, I'll be okay," he said and I smiled at hearing his voice more confident and strong.

I then took my hand away from Chris', against my will, and back to the steering wheel. I started the car and then drove him home. I saw that Chris was more relaxed in the seat than he had been when he first got in the car and I mentally commended myself for partly fixing our relationship. "So when are you going out with Katie?" he asked me and my good mood instantly vanished. God, why did I have to ask her out? So what if I'd freaked out for a while, I shouldn't have asked a girl out just because I didn't know what was going on with me.

"Friday night," I replied and he nodded.

"She's pretty," he said and I nodded but frowned slightly. I hated that it sounded like Chris was forcing this conversation...but I wouldn't blame him. Why would he want to talk about my current girlfriend when I'd slept with him only 2 days ago?

When we reached his house I parked the car in his driveway and climbed out. Chris opened his door but was struggling to lift himself out. I ran around the car and put my arms around him and lifted him out. "You really should tell the principal," I told him but he stubbornly shook his head.

"I've got less than a year," he said. "I can cope with that." I didn't know why he wouldn't tell anyone about it. I guessed Jared had threatened him because Chris isn't normally scared to do something he knows is right. I sighed and helped him get inside his house. Both his parents were at work so the house was empty. "Where?" I asked him.

"Bedroom," he said then quickly stopped. "No! Um, living room." I frowned slightly and then realized he was too uncomfortable to be in his bedroom with me again. I bit my lip before helping him into the living room. I set him on the sofa and he fell onto his back, groaning as he did so.

"What did the nurse say?" I asked as I watched his face contract in pain.

"Severely bruised but not broken," he replied and I nodded, relieved. I sat next to his head and softly stroked his hair before I realized what I was doing. I felt him tense but he quickly relaxed again as I continued. "TV?" I asked and he nodded. I found the remote and turned it on. I heard Chris sigh softly and he snuggled further into the sofa. I lifted my hand off his head for a second and he shifted so his head was resting on my leg. I briefly wondered if he realized he'd done that but I didn't give him the opportunity to move away before I continued to stroke his soft black hair. I smiled as I watched Chris' eyes shut tiredly. "Tired, baby?" I whispered, my stomach twisting when I realized what I called him. However, Chris just nodded slightly, too tired to realize my slip up.

Despite the fact that the television was on, my eyes were glued to Chris' sleeping face for over an hour, until his parents came home, waking him up when they closed the door behind them.

Chapter 11

I jerked awake when I heard the door shut and realized I had my head in Justin's lap. I gasped and quickly sat up, groaning when I put weight on my ribs. "Idiot," Justin said. I turned to him but saw him smirking and I grinned and shrugged. I was glad he seemed to be back to normal. He wasn't awkward anymore, just himself.

"Boys?" I heard mum ask and I turned to see her and dad walk into the room. "What are you doing home so early?" I raised my head properly and she gasped and rushed over to me. "Chris, what happened!?"

"It's nothing, mum," I replied, not wanting her to make a big deal about it. "Who was it?" dad asked from across the room. I glanced at him but then looked away.

"Chris, you have to report this! This is the 5th time in the last *month* that you've come home because someone did this to you!" I nodded at my mum's words but didn't really listen. I already knew how many times Jared beat me up every month, and it was more than she realized. I normally could hide it from her and dad. I heard mum sigh and she turned away. "I'll start dinner," she said and I nodded. "I'm guessing you're staying, Justin?" mum asked.

"Um, sure, thanks," he smiled and I smiled slightly as well. I looked down and realized we were holding hands. I don't know when that had happened or how, but it felt so natural and right that I wasn't going to take my hand away from his.

My dad came and sat in an armchair and took the remote from Justin and turned the channel to what he wanted to watch. I met Justin's eye and saw he was trying not to laugh. I rolled my eyes, smirking slightly and then stood up slowly. "We'll be upstairs if you need us," I said to my dad, who just nodded. I looked at Justin and saw he was looking at me in shock. I frowned slightly, wondering why he would be surprised at the suggestion. We always spent most of the time in my room anyway. I was about to suggest something else because it seemed like Justin didn't want to go to my room, but Justin quickly jumped up and headed out of the room. I frowned slightly but then shook my head and followed him. I got to the bottom of the stairs, lifted my foot onto the first step and pain ricocheted through my torso. I bit my lip and carried on, putting weight on my leg and pulling myself forward. I couldn't help a small whimper to pass my lips. Justin, who had reached the top by this time, quickly stopped and turned around. It took him less than a second to realize what was wrong and then he quickly ran back down the stairs.

"What can I do to help?" he asked me and I reached up, grabbed his shirt and pulled him next to me. He automatically wrapped his arm around my waist and practically lifted me up the stairs.

Once we reached the top I turned and grinned at him. "Thanks," I said happily, despite the pain I was still in. Justin just nodded while smiling.

"I think we...uh, you...need to wash your cuts on your face...just in case they get infected or something," he said, inspecting the few cuts on my face. I nodded, frowning slightly when he changed from 'we' to 'you'.

"Can you help?" I asked him, hoping that he wanted me to ask him that. He grinned and nodded and I knew I'd made the right decision. I realized vaguely that I was having to put in a conscious effort to read what Justin was saying, and that saddened me slightly. But the fact that I was still getting it right was comforting.

Instead of going to my room, we went straight to the bathroom. I went and looked through the cupboard for some gauze and disinfectant. I bit my lip because I knew this was going to hurt. I turned back to Justin and held it out in front of me. "You do it," I said. "I'll wimp out if I have to do it to myself." Justin smiled and nodded and came and took the objects from me. I sat on the counter next to the sink and watched as Justin put a fair amount of disinfect on the cloth. He then turned to me and moved closer. I felt my heart skip a beat as he stood between my legs, holding my chin tenderly in his hands. I kept my eyes lowered, scared of what I would find when I looked into Justin's eyes.

"Ready?" he asked and I closed my eyes as I nodded. Justin carefully turned my face and pressed the cloth against the cut on my left cheekbone. I hissed in a breath through my gritted teeth.

"Fuck," I gasped, trying to pull away from the stinging. Justin's grip tightened on my chin, keeping me in place. He took the material away and then dabbed it back on again lightly. I gritted my teeth and held my breath as Justin moved to my lip. I could taste the disinfectant and the sharp smell flooded my nose. I backed away further, breaking away from Justin's hold and took a fresh breath.

"Sorry," Justin said. I turned back to him and looked up into his eyes. My breath caught in my throat and I couldn't look away from his enchanting blue eyes. I found myself leaning forward, wanting desperately to touch him, to kiss him. He didn't lean away, just continued to stare into my eyes. As I got only inches apart I realized what I was about to do – ruin our friendship – and I quickly leaned back away and looked down.

Only a second passed before Justin put his hand under my chin and raised my head again. For a heart-stopping second I thought he was going to kiss me, but then he raised his hand and pressed the cloth back to my cut. I winced slightly but continued to look into his eyes and the pain seemed more bearable. I wondered if he knew I was going to kiss him, it would be hard not to realize, but he didn't seem freaked out by it. It hadn't made him uncomfortable. I bit my lip slightly to stop from smiling.

Chapter 12

After I had finished cleaning Chris' cuts I moved away from him. I was slightly disappointed that he hadn't closed the distance between us and kissed me, but I had accepted that he hadn't. He thought I was straight. He thought I was happily going out with Katie. He thought I didn't want to kiss him. "How are your ribs?" I asked him. He shrugged slightly. I moved my hands onto his sides, running my hands down his sides, over his bruised bones. I looked up into his eyes and met his intense gaze. I smiled slightly and he returned it.

"I'm okay," he said and I nodded. We walked back to his room and I glanced at the bed. He had changed the sheets, not that I blame him, and all the evidence was gone. As though it never happened. I frowned slightly, wondering if that was Chris' wish – that it had never happened. I turned and looked at Chris and felt myself freeze. He had taken his shirt off and was looking through his closet in search of a new one. I glanced at the shirt he had just taken off that was on the floor and realized that it had blood over it and that was why he had taken it off. My eyes scanned over his smooth back, wishing I could go to him and hold him. I bit my lip but couldn't force myself to look away. After finding a shirt, Chris turned back around and I couldn't contain a gasp. It wasn't because of his chest, which was a sight on its own, but because of the horrid black bruises on his ribs.

"Chris..." I whispered. How could he play down this pain? It would be constantly hurting him. I moved towards him and gently ran my fingertips down his sides. I felt him shiver slightly. "I'm so sorry, Chris," I whispered and pulled him tightly against me. I just needed to hold him, to make sure he was okay. And when he was in my arms, I believed that he was okay.

The rest of the week past slowly. I was glad to see that the relationship between myself and Chris was pretty much back to normal, even though I was very aware of the tension between us when we got too close.

Eventually, Friday arrived and I was regretting my decision to go out with Katie even more than I had previously. "Where are you taking her?" Chris asked me Friday lunch just after Katie had walked away.

"Cinema?" I asked him. I hadn't really put much thought into it, but to be honest, I didn't really care. I looked at Chris to see him smirking slightly.

"Don't put in too much of an effort," he said sarcastically and I shrugged.

"You don't like her," he said. He didn't have to ask, he knew. I shrugged again. "Why are you going out with her? Why did you ask her?" I looked up into his eyes. I wanted to shrug again but I didn't need to. I did know my answer; I just didn't want him to know it. I think Chris knew my answer, but neither of us said anymore.

The end of the day arrived soon and Katie came skipping over to me. I smiled at her and she grinned at me. "I'll pick you up at 7 okay?" I asked her and she nodded.

"See you later," she said and pecked me on the lips before hurriedly walking away to join her friends. I turned to Chris to see he had raised an eyebrow and was looking at me questioningly. I decided to ignore him and we continued to walk to his car. We both got in and I waited for Chris to start the car but he didn't.

"Why are you going out with her?" he asked me. It was the same question from before but his teasing tone had vanished to be replaced with despair. I turned to him, my eyes sad and met his gaze. Only then did I really see how much I was hurting him, and it killed me. I wanted to apologize, but that would give away my feelings towards him. And I couldn't do that, not yet. Instead, I said nothing and Chris turned away and started the car. The drive home was silent, neither of us speaking because neither of us wanted to speak about what was going through our heads.

Once we got back to his house, I got out the car and turned to Chris. I didn't want to, but I knew I had to go home and get ready.

"I'll see you tomorrow, yeah?" I asked him. He turned to me and I noticed his eyes had a red rim around them, as though he was trying hard not to cry. "Chris, I...I..." I wanted to say something, to try to make him understand why I had to do this. But no words came out because I knew that what I was doing had no excuse. I was hurting Chris, and in the process, myself. I looked into his eyes for what felt like an eternity and then I turned and walked away.

Chapter 13

I watched as Justin walked away and silent tears fell down my cheeks. I wanted desperately for him to come back, to tell me that he didn't really want to go out with Katie, that he wanted *me*. I could lie to myself all I wanted, pretending that Justin really did like me as I liked him, but in reality... In reality, Justin was **straight**; Justin was going out with Katie, a girl. In reality, Justin wasn't in love with me.

I squeezed my eyes shut, forcing my tears back, and then walked inside. Neither of my parents were home, so I could get up to my room and suffer on my own, with no one coming and asking me what was wrong. I went and fell down on my bed, burying my face in my pillow and cried my eyes out. I'd always known there was no hope for me and Justin, but after last Saturday, I'd foolishly told myself that there might be. That maybe Justin was gay...or at least confused about his sexuality. I'd hoped that he was, that he would come to me, talk to me about it. But no, I was just someone he could sleep with. And the pain that ran through my heart when that realization hit me was more than I could bear. I felt the pain of a thousand heartbreaks and didn't know how I would ever get over it.

I lay there for what felt like hours, crying into my pillow for what could have been between me and Justin.

I don't know how much later it was that there was a timid knock at my door. I frowned and lifted my head from my wet pillow. I glanced at my clock and saw it was 7.30. Justin would be on his date now, he would have picked her up half an hour ago and would be sitting with her now. My stomach churned as I realized this and I thought I was going to be sick.

There was another knock and I realized that the person outside was still waiting for my reply.

Despite the fact that I knew it wouldn't be, a small part of me still had hope that it would be Justin, coming to me to admit that he couldn't do it.

"Yeah?" I called out and my door opened. My stomach tightened in anticipation and then dropped when I saw my mum walk through the door. She smiled sadly at me as she sat next to me. I then realized that she would have been home for a few hours. She would have heard me crying but she had stayed away. I sat up and wrapped my arms around her and leaned on her shoulder.

"What's wrong, baby?" she asked and I shook my head.

"He...he's on a date..." I said sadly. "I really thought that he...and I... I mean...I..." I closed my eyes tightly, not wanting to cry anymore but knowing that I would no matter what.

"You love him," she guessed and my heart lurched. I nodded and she hugged me tighter.

"I love him so much," I whispered and I shook my head again. "I guess we just weren't meant to be. No matter what I do...he's just going to think of me as a friend. Always just a friend..." Mum didn't know what to say so she just resorted to holding me tightly and rocking my back and forth, trying to comfort me but not succeeding.

I pulled away from her slowly and looked out the window. It was starting to rain, which I found ironically fitting. "I'm going for a walk," I said. I noticed that my voice sounded hollow, distant, but I didn't know what to do about it. That was how I was feeling now.

"Now? But it's raining, sweetie," she said and I nodded. Instead I just stood and left my room without looking back or saying anything more to my mum.

Chapter 14

Fuck. This was such a fucking disaster. I barely even knew Katie and even she could tell something was wrong with me. Her frequent, 'are-you-okay's' were driving me insane. I just wanted to shout, "no, I am not fucking okay because instead of being with the boy I love, I am here with you!" But I controlled myself and forced a smile to myself and said, "Of course." She always smiled back happily, but then only minutes later she would ask again. I knew I'd brought this upon myself but that didn't stop me from hating the situation I was in.

I had borrowed my mum's car to get us to and from the town center. I was beyond glad that I'd persuaded my mum into letting me take her car because, by the time we left the theatre, it was pouring with rain. Miserable ending to a miserable evening, I thought glumly. I felt vaguely guilty for the crappy date I had given Katie, but not guilty enough to want to prolong it to try to make it better. So we quickly ran to my car and jumped in, shutting the doors on the torrential rain. "Justin, are you sure you're okay?" Katie asked again and I turned to her.

"Why do you ask?" I said instead of replying with my usual answer.

"I don't know...you just seem to be...elsewhere," she said. "Like you don't really want to be here." I looked down, feeling genuinely guilty.

"I'm sorry," I said. "I...I shouldn't have asked you out. It was wrong of me. Truth is...I'm in love with someone else." To her credit, Katie smiled. I looked at her, waiting for her to shout at me, to get angry with me, but it never came.

"I figured," she nodded and I frowned.

"What?" I asked, confused.

"It's pretty obvious," she said. "You asked me out to get over them." She wasn't asking but I nodded anyway.

"I'm sorry," I said again. "I really am."

"It's okay," she smiled. "Why don't you take me home and then go and find this girl and tell her how you feel. A great guy like you, she's bound to feel the same way." My head snapped up and I looked at her. She didn't know *who* I loved. She still thought I was straight. But I wasn't going to tell her the truth, just in case that piece of information pushed her over the edge and she finally got angry with me.

"Thank you, Katie," I smiled. "You really are a great girl." Katie grinned and shrugged. I smiled and started the car and then drove Katie back home. When I pulled up outside her house I leaned over and kissed her cheek softly.

"I'll see you at school," she smiled and I nodded. She climbed out, quickly shut the door and then ran to her front door, trying to get as least wet as possible.

I then turned away from her house and drove back to mine. It wasn't too far away, but in the short drive, I made a decision. A decision that I knew would affect the rest of my life. I pulled into my drive, jumped out of the car, and then ran down the street to Chris' house. I rang the bell three times, desperate to see Chris, to tell him how I felt. I didn't care that I was getting soaked by the rain, I just needed to see him.

I was kind of shocked when Chris' mum, Claire, opened the door. I don't know why I had expected Chris to open the door, but I didn't let it faze me. "Can I speak to Chris please?" I asked her quickly.

"He's not here," she said. I saw a slight frown on her face as she spoke to me but I didn't question it.

"Where is he?" I demanded and her frown deepened. "I have to...I *need* to talk to him. Please!"

"He went for a walk," she said and looked behind me at the rain and shook her head.

"A walk?" I asked, shocked. "It's pouring!" She looked back at me and I realized she didn't need to be told that. "Did he say where he was going?" I asked desperately.

"No," she shook her head. "He left about 3 hours ago. And he didn't take his phone..." It was then that I realized how worried she was.

"I'll find him," I said surely. I didn't know how I could claim that, but I knew I would.

"Justin-" she said but I'd already turned away and was running down the street, desperate to find Chris.

I walked around the labyrinth of roads in our area and didn't find him. Not that I really expected to. If he had been gone for 3 hours, he wouldn't still be on the roads. I decided then to go to the park. It was about an hour's walk away but I didn't care. The fact that it was pitch black, raining like there's no tomorrow and approaching midnight didn't matter to me. I just had to find Chris.

An hour later, I walked through the park gates. The whole place was dark and shadowed, trees creating haunting shapes on the paths and grass. I bit my lip and continued inside cautiously. My mind was chanting, *Please be here. Please be here. Please be here.* If he wasn't here I didn't know where else to check and then I would truly panic. I pushed my hair out of my face for what felt like the millionth time, my long fringe dripping water into my eyes. I continued winding through the trees, straining my ears to hear anything. Lightning suddenly sliced the sky, illuminating the park for a fraction of a second before thunder grumbled loudly, vibrating in my ears. "Fuck," I said as the rain came down with renewed force. But nothing would stop me from finding Chris.

I continued walking and eventually came to a picnic area where there were about 5 picnic tables and several normal park benches. My stomach tightened as I saw a hunched figure sitting on one of the benches. It was Chris. I knew it even from this distance. His head was hung low, water dripping from the end of his nose and chin to the floor. He wasn't moving, he was just sitting there. I moved forward slowly, not wanting to scare him.

I got closer and closer to him and he still didn't react, but I knew he was aware of me. I sat next to him, and he still didn't say anything. "Chris?" I asked and Chris immediately jumped and lifted his head and he stared at me wide-eyed.

"What are you doing here?" he asked and I frowned. He was surprised that it was me.

"Who did you think I was?" I asked him and he shrugged.

"It didn't matter. I didn't care," he said.

"I could have been a murderer or rapist or-"

"I didn't care," he said again, cutting me off and I frowned, worry instantly filling my system. "Why are you here?" he asked me again.

"I...I needed to talk to you," I said. Now that I'd found him, I was scared of what I had to say.

"Really? What about? Your date? How'd it go?" he asked dryly and I scowled, getting slightly angry.

"Fine," I said standing up. "If you don't want to fucking listen to me then I'm not going to fucking talk to you." I went to walk away but Chris' small voice stopped me.

"No," he squeaked out. "Don't go. I'm s-sorry. I just..." He trailed off and shook his head. He stood and walked over to me and hugged me tightly.

"I'm sorry, I didn't mean to snap." I lifted my hands, wrapped one around his waist and the other I buried in his hair. I held him tightly and then took a deep breath and pulled back.

"My date was awful," I said. I looked down into his eyes and saw him frown slightly. I didn't say anything more as I looked at him properly. He was deathly pale, his eyes were red, obviously from crying, and he was soaked to the skin. "I mean, Katie was nice and all. I just...there's someone else I wanted to be with and they weren't there and I was very aware that they weren't there. When they've always been there in the past..." I knew I was babbling but I couldn't just say what I wanted to say. I couldn't just blurt it out. I looked down into his eyes, which had suddenly changed.

"You've *always* been there, Chris," I finished. Chris' eyes widened slightly, but it was hard to do when the rain was pummelling his face so much.

"Chris," I whispered. I'm sure he could hear me over the rain, but he knew what I'd said. He just continued to gaze up at me, staring, waiting for what I was going to say next. "Do you really need me to say it?" I asked but I could see that he did, and so I gave him what he needed. "I love you."

Chapter 15

"I love you," he said and my stomach flipped and my heart soared. He loved me? As in...more than friends? He loved me?

"Seriously?" I asked, needing to make sure.

"I seriously love you," he said and I grinned. I looked into his eyes, which were nearly covered with his wet hair.

"I seriously love you, too," I said. Justin never hesitated before pulling me against him and pressing his lips against mine. I wasn't prepared for the sensation of having Justin's lips touching mine for the first time. I gasped and felt Justin grin into the kiss before taking advantage of my open mouth and deepening the kiss. This wasn't like the kisses we'd shared a week ago, then it had been about sex and lust. Now, it was love and tenderness. And I never wanted it to end. I heard thunder fill the air around us and I guessed the park had momentarily lit up due to lightening, but fireworks were going off on my closed eye lids and I didn't notice anything. I wrapped my arms around his neck and held myself against his body tighter. Despite the fact that he was as wet as I was, his body was warm and my body strained to be closer to his.

"Chris," Justin gasped as he pulled away, trying to catch his breath. "I need to tell you something."

"I need to tell you something, too," I said. I decided that I should tell him about last week. I mean, if we were going to give *us* a try, then I should tell him what happened last week. "We should get home first. Get dry." He nodded, agreeing. But neither of us moved. We both just stayed standing in the rain. I watched the water running down Justin's face and was suddenly tempted to stretch up and follow the path the droplets had taken with my tongue. But I controlled myself and just kissed his lips again. I reached down and took his hand, which had previously been resting on my hip. I threaded my fingers with his and then we started the hour long walk home.

Once we walked through my front door my mum immediately met us with towels. "What the hell were you thinking? You're going to catch your death!" She wrapped us both up and closed the door behind us. I glanced at the clock and saw it was nearly 2 a.m. My mum had waited up for us.

"Thanks mum," I smiled. "And I'm sorry." She looked at me and smiled understandingly.

"It's okay, I'm going to bed now," she said and I smiled and nodded.

"Night," I smiled and she kissed my cheek before going upstairs. I heard her bedroom door shut before I turned back to Justin nervously. How was I going to do this? I looked at him and saw he looked just as nervous as I did. I reached out and took his hand and led him up to my room. I went to my closet and took out two t-shirts and two pairs of boxers and chucked one set at Justin. "Um, I'm going to the bathroom. I'll be back in a second," I said, my cheeks warming slightly before I turned away. I saw Justin smile slightly as I basically ran from the room.

I quickly got changed, hoping that Justin was being quick as well, because all I wanted was to see him again, to make sure this had really happened. I hesitantly walked in, just in case Justin hadn't finished changing yet, but he had and was sitting on my bed patiently waiting for me. I smiled softly and shut my door before crossing the room and sitting on the bed next to him.

"Chris, I..." he started and then bit his lip. "I owe you so many apologies..."

"Justin, I promise you I forgive you for all of them," I said softly, a small smile on my lips. "I understand why you went out with Katie; you were scared. And it's okay." He smiled and looked up into my eyes.

"That's not the worst thing, though," he murmured and I frowned slightly wondering what else he'd done. "Last Saturday..." he whispered and I instantly tensed. What could he remember? "Please don't hate me," he said suddenly, looking into my eyes. I frowned and shook my head, telling him I could never hate him. "Um..." he said and looked away from me frowning. "I don't know how to say this..."

"Just say it," I said softly. I took hold of his hand reassuringly and gave it a squeeze.

"I didn't drink anything at the party," he said and I frowned while my heart started racing.

"What? Yes you did, you were drunk..." I said, confused.

"No I didn't...I..." He looked down and shook his head. Concern flooded me when I saw a tear run silently down his cheek. "I faked it. I wasn't drunk I was pretending because..." He trailed off and I waited in a stunned silence for him to continue. "...because I wanted *you*. I didn't want anyone else at that party, only you. But I couldn't tell you that because...well, I was scared. But that didn't stop me wanting you. And I knew that if I was drunk then I could do what I wanted with an excuse that you would accept." I stared at him, my mouth hanging open. How could he do that to me? I've hated myself for allowing him to sleep with me when I believed he was straight and would hate himself if he found out the truth.

"Why couldn't you tell me?" I asked softly, feeling that I had to say something. "I told you I was gay. Why couldn't you tell me?"
"I-I'm sorry," he whispered. "I was scared. Not of you knowing, but

everyone else..." I didn't reply. I didn't know how to feel. He'd deceived me, he'd manipulated me. And yet, when I looked into his sad blue eyes, brimming with tears, I couldn't find any emotion inside me except love. "I'm so sorry, Chris," he said sadly and he looked down, away from my eyes as though he felt he didn't deserve to meet my eyes.

"Justin...last Saturday was the best night of my life," I said softly. I lifted his chin with my forefinger and looked into his eyes. "And now knowing that you chose to do it. That you wanted *me* and weren't just desperate... You have no idea what that means to me. I know you lied, I do, but...I don't really mind. Of course, I wish you hadn't, but I can't change that you did. But that was still the best night of my life..."

"So far," Justin whispered and I smiled, agreeing.

"So far..." I said. "And I think the latter half of this night comes in a close second." Justin grinned and kissed me deeply. He then pulled away slowly, drawing out the perfect moment. We both then got into bed and Justin pulled me firmly against his chest. He kissed the back of my neck softly and I smiled.

Chapter 16

-Justin-

I lay in the dark for almost an hour. I just couldn't sleep. I didn't understand how Chris could forgive me just like that. I mean, I treated him horribly. "I'm so sorry, Chris," I whispered into his hair. To my surprise, Chris turned around and looked into my eyes, sleep miles away.

"It's okay," he whispered back. "Please don't feel bad, Justin."

"Why aren't you asleep?" I asked him. I was going to feel guilty whether he told me to or not.

"Too much to think about," he smiled. "You?"

"Same," I said softly. "I don't understand why you're not angry with me..."

"I am," he said surely and I frowned and looked into his eyes. I didn't see any anger in his gaze at all. "But my love for you outweighs my annoyance."

"I don't deserve someone like you," I whispered, closing my eyes.

"Well tough, because you've got me," he said. I opened my eyes and met Chris' happy gaze.

"Um, Chris, can I ask you something?" I asked hesitantly.

"Of course," he said.

"Um...I want...there to be an us, obviously, but..." I trailed off, not knowing how to say it.

"You're scared," he said and I looked into his eyes again. I nodded slowly, sadly. I didn't want us to be a secret, but I was scared about how people would treat me once I came out.

"I'm sorry," I said again and Chris smiled.

"Stop apologising," he said. "I don't mind if we have to be a secret. I don't think you realise just how happy you've made me. I've been in love with you for over a year. Just having you is enough for me."

"A year?" I asked. "That's why you didn't date...? *Me...?"* Chris blushed slightly and nodded. "Why didn't you tell me?" Chris looked at me like I was an idiot and I nodded. He thought I was straight. "Chris, I've um, I didn't tell you because I thought you were keeping something from me. I'm sorry, I know it's childish but...I couldn't help it."

"How long have you know you were gay?" he asked me and I bit my lip. "Um, a while," I said softly. "I think...I got thinking when you told me you were gay. And it didn't take me long to realise that...yeah, I was gay."

"But...the girls?" he asked, confused.

"I'm not proud of it, but I needed a cover," I said softly, looking down. "I was scared of people finding out so I dated...probably too much, to hide it." I looked up to see Chris shaking his head slightly. I lowered my head again, thinking he was appalled by my behaviour. Not that it would surprise me if he was. I mean, it was awful the way I acted.

"You should have just told me," he whispered and I looked up into his eyes.

"I know, and I'm sorry," I said softly. Chris shook his head again and moved closer to me and wrapped his arms around me.

"Stop apologising," Chris whispered in my ear, causing shivers to run down my spine.

"So...you don't mind keeping us a secret?" I asked him and he shook his head without pulling away from me.

"As long as we can be like this when we're alone, then I think I can make my peace with it," he smiled and I tightened my arms around him.

"Besides, we're usually quite touchy-feely with each other anyway. So even if we hold hands or something, I doubt anyone would suspect anything." I smiled slightly and nodded.

"I love you so much," I whispered and Chris buried his face into my shoulder.

"I love you, too," he whispered back.

We lay pressed close to each other for another length of time and I still couldn't get to sleep, and I could tell by the way Chris was breathing that he was awake as well. I bit my lip slightly. "Can you not sleep either?" I asked him and he pulled away and looked up into my eyes.

"No," he said softly and I smiled. I lifted my hand and ran my fingertips down his cheek softly. I let my eyes roam all over his beautiful face, taking in every detail. Before I realised it, Chris had closed the gap between us and was pressing his lips against mine tenderly. I moved my arms to his waist and held him tightly to me. I brushed my tongue along his lower lip and he immediately opened his mouth and welcomed me in.

Suddenly, surprising me, Chris pushed me on to my back and straddled my waist, the kiss not faltering once. I smiled into the kiss and pulled him against my chest. As Chris' body moved against mine I could feel myself hardening and I tried hard to not moan. But when Chris pressed his hips against mine, I couldn't hold back my moan of pleasure.

"Fuck, Chris," I whispered, finally breaking the intense kiss. He leant back slightly and looked down at me, his eyes skimming over my face in the same way mine had done to him just minutes before. I watched as Chris smirked before he ground his hips onto mine. I bit my lip hard and brought my hands to Chris' waist. I needed him to stop otherwise we would get too carried away. "Chris, you have to stop," I gasped out. Chris then leant back down, pressing our chests together and he whispered in my ear.

"No." I moaned loudly and Chris kissed me, trying to cover my moans. Chris then moved his hand to the hem of my t-shirt and ran his fingers over my chest, tickling my skin gently.

"How...How are your ribs?" I asked him, my voice catching. Chris frowned slightly and glanced up at me.

"Much better," he said.

"Good," I said and the quickly flipped him so I was lying over him. He stared at me wide-eyed and then a grin grew on his lips. I didn't hesitate before grinding my hips against Chris' cloth-covered erection and this time it was he who moaned. I grinned and reached down and pulled his shirt over his head. I then lowered my head and licked over his chest, sucking his nipples as I went.

"Justin...*God,*"he moaned and I smirked slightly. I moved lower and reached his boxers. I grew slightly nervous; I'd never done this before, but that apprehension didn't stop me from pulling Chris' boxers off him completely. I gasped slightly and looked up at Chris, who was gazing down at me, his eyes glazed with lust. I lowered my head and kissed his stomach and down to his thighs, earning a frustrated moan from Chris.

"Justin, stop teasing me," he whispered. I looked up into his eyes and then lowered my head and kissed the tip of Chris' cock. He moaned and I took the tip into my mouth. I could taste his pre-cum but it didn't put me off. I liked the taste of him. I swirled my tongue over the tip and then pulled away, moving to lick up and down his cock. "Jus..." he gasped and I finally took as much of his as I could into my mouth. He moaned and I started moving my head up and down, sucking gently as I did so. Chris' hands went to my hair and held me tightly. I moaned and the vibrations I made caused Chris' hips to thrust forward into my mouth. I moved my hands to his hips to stop him moving and then tried to take him even deeper into my mouth. I moved faster and he moaned more frequently. "Justin, fuck, I'm gonna-" He threw his head back and moaned, cutting his warning short. I felt his cock swell slightly and then he was coming down my throat. I continued to suck softly until his orgasm had passed and then I pulled back. I sat back on my knees and gazed down at him; he was panting heavily, sweat covered his body, but I had never seen him looking so incredible. "Fuck," Chris whispered once he had caught his breath. I smiled down at him and then he looked up and met my eyes. I saw a smirk grow on his face and he grabbed my shoulders, flipped us over and pinned me down. He leant down and kissed me, brushing his tongue over mine before moving to my ear. "I need you inside me, baby," he whispered and I moaned.

"Fuck, yes," I said, desperate to feel him around me once again. Chris then tore at my clothes until I was just as naked as him. His eyes roamed over my body and he bit his lower lip. I moved my hands to his waist and then slid down and I gently pushed one finger inside Chris' tight hole. I heard him gasp and I slowed my movements, giving him time to get used to it.

"Justin," Chris moaned and I pushed another finger inside him. God, I didn't think I would ever get used to him moaning my name like that.

"Stop, I want..." he whispered, pulling my hand away from him. He then hovered over my cock and slowly sank down onto me. I felt my cock stretching him tight and I knew this would hurt him, but he didn't stop until he was sitting on my hips completely. Chris then leant forward, lying on my chest. I could hear him gasping in breath and I waited for him to become used to my cock inside him. I slowly rubbed his back and eventually, he sat up and rotated his hips slowly. He gazed down into my eyes as he did so and the level of love I saw in his eyes almost brought tears to mine. I took hold of his hand and put it on my chest above my heart, so he could feel it racing. He smiled softly and lifted up my hand and put it on his heart, which was racing just as fast as mine. "I love you," he whispered.

"I love you," I whispered back. He smiled and then raised his hips and brought them back down heavily. I moaned, low in my throat as I felt my cock enveloped in his warmth. "Chris, oh, God..." He then sped up; riding me faster and harder and I felt my orgasm building. Chris suddenly moaned and I realised I'd hit his prostate. I shifted position slightly and aimed to hit it every thrust. I also took hold of Chris' cock and pumped him in time with my thrusts, to help him get off in time with me. Chris' nails dug into my shoulders but I didn't care, all I cared about was how good Chris felt around me right now. My hips started thrusting more erratically and I could feel my orgasm about to arrive. Two more thrusts and I was pushed over the edge. I heard Chris moan as well and I realised that he'd come at the same time. He then collapsed over me, burying his head under my chin. "Do you think we could get some sleep now?" I asked, a small smile on my lips.

"Mmm," he smiled. "I think so."

Chapter 17

When I opened my eyes I smiled when I felt Justin's body pressed against mine. This was a much better waking up than last week. I could feel Justin's chest pressed close to my back and I could feel his soft breath tickling my neck. I turned around carefully and once I was facing him, Justin pulled me tighter to him and I smiled again. He was still asleep, but even when he was unconscious he wanted me close. I leaned my forehead against his softly and closed my eyes and drifted off to sleep again.

When my eyes next opened, I saw Justin millimeters away from me and I felt his lips pressing against mine. I smiled against his lips and then pulled away and looked into his warm eyes. "Morning," I smiled and Justin smiled back.

"Morning," he whispered, leaning his forehead against mine. I lifted my hand and gently stroked his cheek tenderly. He brought his hand up and held my hand as it rested on his cheek. I glanced at the clock and saw it was 1.30. It didn't surprise me that we had slept in so late, especially considering we didn't actually get to sleep until about 5 in the morning... And I still wasn't ready to get up. Instead, I just snuggled closer to Justin and wrapped my arms around him tightly. I felt him sigh contently and hug me back tightly. Neither of us fell asleep again, but we just lay silent in each other's arms. The corners of my lips were permanently lifted in a small smile, and no matter what, it wouldn't go away. My thoughts returned to last night, starting from when Justin had found me in the park. We'd shared our first proper kiss in the park at midnight in the pouring rain. It was all so romantic. I softly pressed my lips against Justin's neck – which was the nearest available piece of skin.

"Love you," I whispered. I didn't intend for him to hear, I just wanted to say the words, but Justin's arms tightened around me.

"Love you, too," he whispered and I smiled.

After a long, calm while we got out of bed. I knew both my parents were out because out of my window I had seen that both of their cars were gone. So Justin and I didn't bother with getting dressed. We went into the kitchen and I pulled out some bread. "Sandwich?" I asked him and he nodded. He got the fillings out of the fridge and then came over to me. We then made our lunch in silence, but it was comfortable and relaxed. We went into the living room to eat and we sat as close to one another as possible. The whole of my right side touched the whole of his left.

The rest of the day we spent just lounging around the house, not doing much, just being together. I smiled but couldn't help but wonder what was going to happen when we got back to school. I didn't even know if Justin would be happy to be together in public – like walking down the street. I looked at him and saw he was smiling softly, contently, as he watched television and I smiled as well. "Justin, what's going to happen on Monday?" I asked him softly, watching his face closely for any change. He managed to keep his expression the same, however, I felt his body tense. He wasn't comfortable being with me in public. Not yet anyway.

"Chris-"

"It's okay," I interrupted, already knowing from his pleading look and tone what he was going to say. "You're not ready yet. It's okay."

"I'm sorry," he said, looking down. I frowned slightly and put my fingers on his chin and lifted his head to face me.

"Justin, you don't have to be sorry," I whispered. "I'm with you, I'm happy. I understand you aren't ready to come out and that's okay. We can be together like this, right?" Justin smiled and nodded.

"Definitely," he said and as if to prove his point, he snuggled closer to me. His hand found mine and gripped it tightly and I smiled softly. I would wait until Justin was ready. I'd rather be with him in secret than not be with him at all. So I just had to make the most of the time we had alone.

Chapter 18

Chris and I spent most of the weekend together. I only went home briefly to change into clean clothes, before heading back to Chris' house. I couldn't get enough of him. I knew that once school started, I would automatically, unintentionally, put a distance between us, possibly more than usual because I would be more paranoid than normal. So I had to make the most of the weekend, I had to show Chris that I wanted him and that what will happen at school doesn't mean anything.

When Monday arrived, Chris picked me up as usual and I grinned when I saw him. I practically ran to his car and jumped in. I kissed him tenderly even before I closed the door behind me. "Hey," he smiled and I grinned.

"Hi," I said happily.

"Ready for school?" he asked and I hesitated and looked at him. He looked anxious, nervous, and I knew why. He didn't know how to act around me, pretending that we weren't together. I bit my lip slightly and reached over and took his hand.

"Chris, I..." I trailed off, not sure how to say what I wanted to say. "I know this is going to be hard. But just try, please. That's all I'm asking. If something goes wrong, and people guess, then I'll just have to get over it. But, please, for now just try to pretend." He looked into my eyes and then nodded, looking down. "Chris?" I asked softly, hoping he wouldn't be too angry with me.

"It's okay," Chris said softly, nodding slightly. "I've pretended I wasn't in love with you for the last year...what's another couple of months?" I didn't say anything; I didn't know how to respond to his bitter tone. He sighed then and turned to me. "I'm sorry," he said softly. "I just...I thought that once I had you...we would be together."

"We *are* together," I said insistently.

"Yeah," he sighed. He went to start the car, but I put my hand on his chin and turned him back to face me. I looked into his eyes and saw how upset he was.

"You know how much I love you, right?" I whispered and he nodded.

"I know," he said softly. He moved into my arms and I held him tightly, never wanting to let go. He clutched at my shirt tightly in his fists. "I love you, too." He pulled away then and started the car. All I wanted to do was to pull him back against me, but I didn't. Instead, I spent the short journey, just looking at him. Making sure he really was alright.

When Chris had parked, he turned to me and smiled. "You know, that was kinda creepy," he said and I frowned, confused. "You staring at me," he elaborated and I grinned, glad that Chris seemed to be happy again. "I don't care if it's creepy," I grinned as I opened the door. "I'm gonna stare at you whether you like it or not." I then got out of the car before Chris could reply. Chris then got out as well and locked the doors behind him. We walked towards the school building side by side, yet not touching.

"Hey," Zoe said as we reached her and Jake.

"Hey, what's up?" I asked them.

"Not much," Zoe said.

"I don't want to go to Bio..." Jake sighed and I laughed slightly as his pouting expression. Zoe rolled her eyes and poked him in the side.

"Grow up will you?" she asked him and he grinned as he wrapped his arm around her tightly.

"Never," he smiled. "You know that's what you love about me..." Zoe grinned and kissed him softly.

"I guess..." she sighed as they pulled apart. I smiled softly, wanting desperately to reach out and take Chris' hand. I wanted us to be like that. It was only then that I realized Chris was no longer standing next to me. I frowned slightly and looked around, to see Chris' back, moving further and further away from me. "What's with him?" Zoe asked me and I shook my head, indicating that I didn't know. But I *did* know; I could barely stand witnessing Zoe and Jake being so blatantly couply, but it was *my* decision that stopped Chris and myself from being like that. Chris didn't have the same determination I had. All he had was his promise to me. And being around Zoe and Jake must have been hard, knowing...thinking that I didn't want to be with him like that.

I wanted to go after Chris, to comfort him, but I knew there was nothing I could say that would cheer him up. All I could do was apologize, but I don't think that's what Chris would want to hear. And I couldn't say to him what he wanted to hear. I sighed and looked at the floor as I headed to my first class.

Chapter 19

-Chris-

Why did Zoe and Jake have to be so damn cute? I mean, I know they're in love, and that they're together, but why did they have to kiss right then? Why couldn't they have waited until we weren't around? I know, it's not like I usually mind, so there's no reason why I wouldn't want to be present when they act all lovey-dovey, but still... Being with Justin when they were being couply, was just so frustrating. I wanted, more than anything, to be like that with Justin. But I knew I wouldn't be, not for a long while. Justin was scared. And I didn't blame him for being scared. I mean, he's witnessed some pretty nasty things happen to me because I am gay. So why would he want to subject himself to that...for me? I mean, obviously, I'm not worth being subjected to random people's judgment. Obviously Justin cares more about other people's opinions of him, than he does me. Obviously Justin would rather hide from people like Jared, than come out and face the world with me at his side.

I kicked the wall as I forced myself into a deeper depression. I had to stop thinking. I had to turn off my head. I kicked the wall again, harder, and bit back a curse. Fuck, okay, that hurt. I felt my foot throb as I continued walking towards my English class. I took a deep breath before entering the room. I saw Justin was already there and I smiled at him slightly. He smiled back and I could see the worry and sadness in his eyes. I sat down in the chair next to him as usual and he reached under the table and took my hand in his. I looked up into his eyes. "Are you okay?" he asked and I shrugged.

"Of course," I said, my tone alone telling him I was anything but.

"Why are you limping?" he asked and I frowned slightly.

"I hurt my foot," I said. Justin didn't say anything, just waited for me to elaborate. "I kicked the wall. Harder than I realized." To my surprise, Justin snorted and shook his head. "What?" I asked. I wanted to be annoyed that he was laughing at my pain, but my lips pulled upwards slightly at the noise he had made. "What's so funny?" I asked, my smile clear in my voice now.

"You kicked the wall...such a normal thing to do," he grinned and I shrugged again.

"Felt normal at the time," I said, defending my actions.

"Sure..." he said, drawing out the vowels. I just rolled my eyes and turned away from him. He gave my hand a final squeeze under the desk, and then brought his hand up to rest on the tabletop. I frowned slightly, feeling the loss of Justin's hand around mine.

The lesson passed agonizingly slowly, I just wanted school to finish so Justin and I can be together again. At lunch I had a shock when Katie came over, smiling at Justin, and sat down on his other side. "So did you talk to her?" she asked Justin and I frowned deeper. I tried not to show that I was eavesdropping, so I picked absentmindedly at my food. But I knew Justin knew I was listening in.

"Yeah, we talked," he said to her and, if possible, her grin grew.

"And...?" she asked. "How did it go?"

"Um, good," Justin smiled.

"Aww," Katie cooed. "I told you she'd like you back."

"Yeah," Justin said. I could tell he was somewhat uncomfortable with the conversation, but I don't think Katie realized, because she kept asking him questions. About what Justin said, whether he kissed the girl, whether she kissed back. And more. I just sat quietly, listening to Justin and Katie talking about this girl. Well, Katie was talking about a girl, Justin was talking about me. *I* was Justin's girlfriend. My hand which was resting on my lap clenched. I didn't want to be Justin's mysterious girlfriend. I wanted to be Justin's boyfriend. And not just in secret. I wanted to be Justin's boyfriend in public.

"Chris? You okay?" I looked up and saw Zoe and Jake were looking at me, Zoe having asked the question.

"You don't look very good, man," Jake said. At this, I heard Katie and Justin stop talking about our kiss in the rain.

"I'm fine," I mumbled.

"Do you need to go to the nurse?" Zoe asked me, concerned.

"No, I'm fine you guys, I promise," I said, standing up. I met Justin's eyes briefly before I turned away. But the desperation in his eyes made my heart cry. "I'm, um, going to the bathroom." I quickly cleared my tray and left the cafeteria.

Instead of going to the bathroom, I went outside and sat on a wall. I took deep breaths of the air. The day was hot and humid after the thunderstorm last night. But I didn't care that the air was thick and heavy, I just wanted to be away from Justin and Katie. Actually, I just wanted to get away from Justin. The temptation to touch him, to be possessive of him, was just too strong.

I felt a hand rest suddenly on my shoulder and I jumped and turned around. "You okay, sweetie?" Zoe asked and I smiled and nodded, turning back to looking over the sports fields. "What's wrong?" she asked me, sitting down next to me. To her credit, she sat down where I couldn't see her, so it didn't seem like she was forcing herself into my problems. "Justin," I sighed, looking down. "He, um...we...um..." I trailed off, not knowing how to tell one of my best friends that one of her best friends is gay.

"You're together?" she asked and I nodded, looking up in confusion.

"Chris, it may have taken Justin years to realize, but I've always known that you were in love with him. I'm glad Justin finally accepted it."

"But he hasn't," I said. "That's the problem. He hasn't accepted that he's gay...he's just accepted that he loves me. He doesn't want us to be...*together.* Not properly anyway. He's scared, and I understand that it's just...I've wanted him for so long. And now I've got him, it's like he doesn't want me to have him. He's scared of what people will do if they find out he's gay. And I understand that too because he's seen what people do to me. I just...I don't know..." I didn't realize that tears were on my cheeks until a droplet fell from my chin and landed on my hand. I quickly brushed my tears away and stood up, shaking my head. "I just have to be patient...and ignore things everyone says to him."

"So, this is about what Katie was saying?" Zoe asked and I turned to her.

"Only partly," I said. "How can he just lie like that?"

"He wasn't lying," Zoe said. "I could see in his face. That story he told her was true, wasn't it? Everything he said was true; he just changed the 'he' to a 'she'."

"That's a big change, though," I said softly. "The story was true, I'll give you that. But that's not the point. He's okay with sharing what we do together, as long as no one finds out it's me he does it with..."

"Chris," she said but I just shook my head.

"I'm skipping the final period," I said. "I'm going to sit in the common room or something. I don't want to go to class."

"Chris!" she tried again but I just walked away. I was in no mood to be in a lesson, I wouldn't learn anything. I was glad that I didn't have this class with Justin because I knew he would come looking for me if I didn't turn up and then I'd be forced to tell him why I was upset. And I wasn't going to do that. I told him I'd wait until he was ready to come out, and that's what I'm going to do.

Chapter 20

I still didn't understand why Zoe had thought it would be better for her to go and talk to Chris. But I couldn't tell her why I wanted to talk to him, why I *needed* to talk to him. So I had unhappily agreed to let her go and talk to my boyfriend. However, after about 2 minutes I couldn't stand it and I quickly left the cafeteria. The only problem was that I didn't know where they would be. I wondered around for a short while and then, when I walked through the main entrance, I saw they were sat on the wall outside. I frowned slightly and moved towards them. Both of them were looking in the opposite direction to me, so I edged closer until I could hear them...until I could hear Chris crying. His words brought tears to my eyes. I really wasn't being fair to him at all. I hated the way I was acting, the way I was treating him. I wished I had the courage, and the strength to give Chris what he wanted. But I just couldn't. I wish someone could just do it for me, but I couldn't just ask someone to do it – that would be weird, for one thing, and cowardly for another. No, this was something I had to do. But fuck, I didn't want to do it.

I moved away from Chris and Zoe silently and went to class. I didn't learn anything throughout the whole lesson, I was thinking about things that were so much more important than algebra. This was my life, for crying out loud. I decided during that lesson that I needed to go out this weekend, and get drunk. I needed, momentarily, to forget about all that was going on in my life. Well, all the bad stuff.

At 4 o'clock, when school ended, I slowly made my way to Chris' car. He was already inside, waiting for me. I climbed in and smiled at him, pretending that nothing was wrong. "Hey," I smiled and Chris smiled back.

I wanted to lean across and kiss him, but kids were constantly walking past the car to get to their destinations, so it was likely that we would be seen. Instead, I just reached down and took hold of Chris' hand. I heard him sigh softly and wondered if it was a happy sigh, or a sad sigh. I hoped it was a happy sigh, but knew that it would more likely be a sad sigh.

"Let's go home," he said softly and I nodded, taking my hand away. Chris quickly reversed the car out of the space and then drove out of the school and started the short distance back to his house.

Once Chris had parked in his drive, we both got out of the car, still in silence. I bit my lip, wondering what I was going to say to him, wondering how I could make him feel better. I didn't even realize we were inside his house until I felt his soft lips pressing against mine. My eyes closed and I immediately kissed back. "God, I've wanted to do that all day," he whispered against my lips as he pulled away.

"Really?" I asked unsurely.

"Of course," he said, frowning. "Why wouldn't I?"

"I thought you were upset with me..." I said, confused. "For...the whole secret thing..." I saw him look down and bite his lip.

"I was...but...I love you," he said, as though that explained everything.

"And as much as I want to be with you. I want you to be happy... And...you're happy with no one knowing about us."

"No," I said quickly, hating the way he phrased it. I wasn't *ashamed* that I was with him. "I'm happy with no one knowing about *me.* And unfortunately, that now includes you. I would never be happier than when everyone knows about us, about the love we share. But I'm not ready for everyone to judge me. Not yet." He looked up at me, frowning slightly.

"So...you want people to know we're together?" he asked. "You're just not ready to come out..." I frowned slightly at how badly I'd explained it. "I don't want to hide my love for you," I whispered, gently running my fingertips over his cheek. "Unfortunately, if I don't hide it, people may...react badly." Chris nodded, even though I still didn't think I was making much sense. "Chris, I really do love you," I said and he looked up into my eyes.

"I know you do," he whispered as he moved closer into my arms. "No matter what happens, I'm not letting you go." I smiled softly and tightened my arms around him, trying to hold him as close as possible.

Chapter 21

The rest of the week past uneventfully. Justin didn't change his mind about us remaining a secret, but as the days passed I was slowly becoming more and more used to it. I knew that I could act however I wanted around Justin when we were on our own. But in front of everyone else, we were just friends. Even though it's not how I imagined our relationship to be, I had to accept it. If I wanted Justin, and I did, I just had to suck it up. At least until he was ready to come out.

However, there was one problem with Justin's plan. As no one knew we were together, no one knew that Justin was no longer single. Which meant that an endless stream of girls was talking to him, flirting with him. It was nothing new. I mean, girls had always acted that way around him. But that had been when I thought he was straight. When we weren't together. But I couldn't say anything. I couldn't tell these girls to *back the fuck away from my boyfriend.* And Justin didn't say anything either. Well, he told them he wasn't interested, but not *why.* And without any decent explanation, these girls just kept trying. Not that I was worried about anything happening between Justin and these girls, because I knew Justin loved me... It just hurt to see Justin with girls who were obviously hitting on him.

I hadn't told Justin that I'd told Zoe about him and me. I didn't want to tell Justin that I hadn't been able to keep his secret. I don't think he would mind anyway, but I didn't want to tell him in case he was annoyed I'd said something.

We were in the common room after lunch, just before our last lesson on

Friday when my mobile rang. "Hello?" I said. I was glad for the distraction from watching Justin talking to this girl whose name I didn't know.

"Chris Adams?" a voice said and I frowned slightly.

"Yes?" I replied. Something settled inside me and my heart started racing.

"I'm afraid I have some bad news for you," the person said. Dread settled in the pit of my stomach like a lead weight.

"Who are you?" I asked. I saw Justin, Zoe, and Jake all look over at me but I ignored them.

"Detective Johnston," the man said. A policeman. Why was a policeman phoning me? "There's been an accident..." He continued talking and the more he said, the more numb I became. Everyone was still staring at me. I could see the concern in their faces, especially Justin's but I didn't say anything to them. I just continued to listen to the detective's story. "...Your father is currently at the hospital with your mother. And I suggest you make your way down there."

"What...what's going to happen?" I asked, my voice weak.

"It's uncertain," Detective Johnson replied. "And I don't know the details of your mother's condition. You can ask the doctor when you get to the hospital. Your father asked me to phone you to ask you to go down there."

"Okay," I said and then closed my phone. I didn't think to say thank you, or goodbye. I was numb. I wasn't thinking. At least...not about manners.

"Chris?" I heard Justin ask. I ignored him and just stood up. "Chris?" I heard Justin call as I walked away towards the doors.

I walked through the doors but they didn't have time to close before they were pushed open again. "Chris!" Justin shouted and he grabbed onto my shoulder and forced me to stop.

"Get off!" I shouted, breaking free of his grip. I started running to the car park and I knew Justin was right behind me. I reached my car after what felt like hours. I just needed to get to the hospital.

"Chris! No way am I fucking letting you drive," he shouted and I turned and glared at him.

"You're not going to fucking stop me," I said and opened the door.

"Chris! Stop!" Justin shouted and grabbed the keys from my hand, and hiding them behind his back.

"Justin! For fuck's sake! Give me the fucking keys!" I shouted, grabbing his jacket. I saw Justin's eyes widen slightly. Not in fear or confusion. In realization. He suddenly realized that this was serious, that I wasn't just leaving school. I wanted to go somewhere.

"I'll drive you," he said. I couldn't argue. Inside I knew that I was in no fit state to drive.

"Fine," I muttered, walking around to the other side of the car.

"Where to?" he asked as he started the car. I bit my lip, frowning. This is why I didn't want Justin, or anyone, to drive me there. I didn't want to say anything.

"The hospital," I said, my voice low and quiet.

"What? Why?" he asked and I turned and glared at him.

"Just do it!" I shouted. Justin flinched but nodded and reversed out of the car park space and out of the school.

I knew I'd hurt Justin, but to be honest, I didn't care. At that moment, all my concerns were focused on my mum.

Chapter 22

I didn't say anything as Chris ran to his dad. I just stood to the side, unsure if I should leave. I'd followed Chris inside, followed him through the hallways where the receptionist had instructed him to go. But now he was crying in his dad's arms and I didn't know what to do. I didn't know if he wanted me here still. I didn't even know what was going on. I looked at Chris' dad, Sean, and saw he had silent tears trickling down his cheeks. I'd known Sean since I was a child and he'd always seemed to be a very well together, dignified man. And he was trying to be strong now, for his son, but he was still crying. I frowned. Something was very, very wrong.

"Mr. Adams?" I turned to see a nurse coming through the waiting room door behind me. Chris and his dad pulled apart and Sean cleared his throat, trying to recompose himself. "Excuse me, sir, I need you to sign some papers," she continued. Sean nodded and went to follow the nurse. I looked at Chris. He watched his dad leave and I felt my heartbreak. He looked so lost. So alone. *No,* I thought. *He's never alone.* I walked over to him and took him into my arms. He briefly hesitated before wrapping his arms around me tightly. His arms kept tightening as I felt his body becoming weaker. He couldn't support himself. I frowned, worried, and held him tighter. He clenched my shirt in his fists. I felt the front of my shirt getting wet and I realized that Chris was shaking, crying.

"Chris," I whispered, soothingly. I moved to the seats that lined the wall and sat down, pulling Chris into my lap. I didn't say anything; I didn't try to reassure him, because I knew he wouldn't believe what I said anyway and it would simply frustrate him. I just held him close, comforting him with my presence.

"What if...what if she..." he whispered in between his tears. Suddenly it hit me. I don't know how I could be as stupid as to miss it. *His dad was crying.* His mum... I didn't know what to say. I could say 'she's going to be fine' because I had no idea what had happened and I wasn't going to lie to him.

I heard someone coming down the hallway and I looked up to see Sean enter the room. He didn't have tears on his cheeks anymore, but he was pale and seemed deflated. He sat next to me but didn't say anything.

"What happened?" Chris asked him, peeking out from my chest.

"She was hit when she was crossing the road by someone on their cell phone," his dad said. His voice sounded detached from what he was saying. I tightened my arms around Chris when I felt him shaking. "She's in surgery at the moment...trying to get the internal bleeding to stop."

Chris moved himself closer to me and I rested my head on top of his. I could hear his breathing, fast and short, and worried he was going to have a panic attack. I rubbed my hand up and down his back in a slow, calm rhythm and I felt his breathing changing, slowing down again.

A silence settled amongst us as we waited for something, anything, to happen. Chris didn't move from my lap, although he did pull away slightly. He shifted so he was sitting sideways on my lap, his head resting on my shoulder. I kept my arms around him, not wanting to let him move any further away from me. I kept checking him, looking down at him to make sure he was okay. He was just staring at nothing, his gaze fixed on the white wall but seeing nothing. I wanted something to happen to snap Chris out of this state; I didn't like seeing him like this. I heard the door open and I looked up to see the doctor. His face wasn't promising.

Sean stood, still hopeful, not reading the doctor's expression. "I'm so sorry," the doctor said and I felt my own heartbreak. Chris' grip tightened on my shirt and he buried himself in my chest again. Sean seemed to be frozen. The doctor was talking, explaining what had happened, what had gone wrong. But none of us were listening. None of us cared. All we cared was that Claire was no longer here. She was gone. I squeezed my eyes shut. I wasn't going to cry because I wanted to be strong for Chris. But Claire had been like a second mum to me. I felt Chris shaking and then he started crying properly. Every sob that passed his lips broke my heart a little more.

"I'm so sorry, Chris," I whispered in his ear. "I'm so, so sorry." He didn't reply, not that I was expecting him to.

"I want to go home," he whimpered.

"Okay, baby, I'll take you home," I said softly. I stood up slowly, Chris standing next to me but still clutching onto me. Sean turned to me. "Chris wants me to take him home," I told him and he nodded.

"I need to sign some more papers," he said. His voice sounded robotic.

"I'll be home in a while." I nodded and then led Chris out of the hospital and back to his car. I still had the keys in my pocket and got them out and unlocked the doors. I opened the door for Chris and then lowered him into the car. Once he was sitting down, he still didn't let go of my shirt.

"Chris," I whispered, taking hold of his hands and pulling slightly. "Let go, baby." His breathing was shaky, but he eventually dropped my shirt. I smiled weakly at him and then closed the door. I quickly walked around the car and got into the driver's seat. I glanced over at Chris to see he had tears streaming down his cheeks. I didn't know what to do, so I put the car in reverse, pulled out of the space, and drove him back to his house as quickly as I could.

Once I'd parked I turned to him. He was looking up at his house and I waited for him to do or say something. He slowly lifted his hand to the handle and opened the door. I jumped out as well and ran around the car and took his hand and pulled him up. I wrapped my arms around him and led him inside his house and up to his room. I lay him on his bed and he pulled me down next to him. "Don't leave me," he whispered and I held onto him tightly.

"Never," I whispered. We lay there for hours, the room slowly getting darker. I knew Chris wasn't asleep because tears were still running freely down his cheeks.

"I k-keep waiting for h-her to come in as-asking i-if we w-want any-anything," he said as he started to cry more. I closed my eyes tightly as I held him closer.

"I know," I whispered, stroking his hair softly.

After a while my phone rang in my pocket, making me jump. Chris shifted slightly so I could get it out and I answered it. "Hello?" I asked. "Justin! Where are you?" mum said worriedly down the phone. I looked down at Chris and saw his eyes were squeezed shut. He knew it was my mum phoning.

"I'm at Chris' house," I said softly. I wanted to explain to her what was going on, but I couldn't with Chris in the room. "I'm staying here tonight..."

"Justin, honey, what's wrong?" she asked. She could hear in my quiet voice that something was wrong. I sat up, making to leave the room but Chris whimpered and clutched at my shirt. I lay back down, pulling Chris against me tightly.

"Chris' mum...was in an accident," I said, trying not to say anything that would get Chris even more worked up.

"Oh, dear, is she alright?" mum asked and I closed my eyes.

"No," I said surely and I heard my mum gasp.

"No..." she whispered and I knew she'd caught on. "Oh, God..."

"I'm staying with Chris tonight," I said, not wanting to talk about it with Chris next to me.

"Of course," she said. "Oh my, God... Poor Sean...poor Chris."

"Mum, I've got to go," I said.

"Of course, bye, sweetie," she said and I hung up. I turned my phone off so it wouldn't ring again and dropped it to the floor next to Chris' bed.

I turned back to Chris and pulled him back against me tightly. "Chris?" I whispered, not liking that he seemed so unresponsive.

"I didn't get to say goodbye," he whispered and tears gathered in my eyes.

"It's not fair."

"I know," I whispered. "I'm so sorry this happened to you, Chris. I'm so, so sorry. I'm going to look after you, okay?" Chris nodded and I was happy to see a weak smile on his lips. "I love you," I whispered, pressing a kiss to his temple.

"I love you," he sighed. We then settled back into silence. I heard the front door open and then close and guessed Sean was home, but neither of us moved. I realized that it was late, but I wasn't going to fall asleep tonight. I wanted to stay awake to ensure that Chris was alright.

Chapter 23

My eyes opened the next morning, but I didn't really feel awake. I rolled over and saw that Justin was still lying next to me, his eyes fixed on me. "It wasn't a dream," I whispered, needing him to confirm it. Justin shook his head sadly. I felt a chill run through my body. My mum was gone. She was gone. Never coming back. What was I going to do? My mum was the person that helped me. She was the one I could always talk to, always go to for advice. I sat up and brought my knees to my chest and leaned my forehead against my knees. "I didn't get to say goodbye," I whispered, tears trickling down my cheeks. Justin sat up next to me and wrapped his arms around me. I didn't lean into his embrace; I just sat staring at the plain blue material on my bed. I didn't know what to do. I felt so lost knowing that my mum wasn't downstairs in the kitchen, knowing that she was never coming back to look after me. "What am I going to do, Justin?" I whispered, needing to just hear his voice, to know that he was here with me, for me.

"I don't know, baby," he whispered. "But I'm not going to let you do it on your own." I smiled weakly and finally leaned into his chest. I didn't uncurl from my position, but Justin didn't seem to mind, he just wrapped his arms around my body and held me tightly.

We sat there for ages, not saying anything. I kept replaying everything that happened yesterday in my head, remembering every detail. "I'm sorry I yelled at you," I whispered, my voice hoarse.

"When?" Justin asked and I buried my face further into his shoulder.

"Yesterday," I whispered. "When you came after me..."

"Oh, baby, it's okay," he whispered, tightening his arms around me. "I love you."

"I love you," I whispered back, my voice wavering beyond my control. Tears ran down my cheeks and I could tell by Justin's slight shaking that he was crying silently as well.

* * * *

Three months later, in mid-march, I still felt the pain as though it had happened yesterday. And I knew Justin was starting to lose patience. Not that he showed me anything but love and consideration, but I just knew he wanted the old me back. It annoyed me that I couldn't give him what he wanted, but I just couldn't. It was too soon.

I'd gone back to school about a month after the funeral. I knew very few people there, but even if I didn't know them, everyone came up to me saying how sorry they were, and how well I was doing being strong to help my dad. If Justin hadn't been there, gripping my hand as tight as I was gripping his, I don't know how I would have stayed there. These people didn't understand what I was going through. None of them understood, none of them had the right to tell me how to behave or how to act. As soon as possible, Justin and I had retreated to my bedroom, hiding from all the people who sported fake smiles. "You did well, baby," Justin whispered. I smiled weakly. I didn't know how I was supposed to act at my mum's funeral. I didn't want anyone to talk to me, but everyone felt as though they ought to. I just wish she was still here to help me through this period. She would know how I was meant to act.

No one at school knew what had happened except Zoe and Jake, and Justin obviously. I didn't want anyone else to know. The teachers had all been told by my dad, but no other students knew. I just wanted this aspect of my life to continue as normal. However, Zoe and Jake treated me very carefully...always watching what they said around me. It was kind of annoying, but I tried to remember that they were just being thoughtful.

A week after I returned to school, I realized that posters were going up for prom, which was taking place in just over a month. I glanced at Justin when I first saw them. If I was going to go I'd want to go with him. But he hasn't come out yet. After everything that's happened, I'd forgotten all about that. But I suddenly remembered that Justin and I weren't actually a couple. Even though Justin was with me all the time, people still didn't know. If we turned up at the prom together...everyone would know Justin was gay. And he didn't want that. Looks like I'm not going to prom then...

Chapter 24

-Justin-

The last couple of months have been...not the worst of my life, but definitely not the best. I know Chris was trying hard to act normal, but I didn't want him to. I wanted him to be upset, I wanted him to cry. I didn't want him to force himself to act like nothing had happened. And the fact that he was doing it for me just hurt all the more.

I was aware that prom was coming up, but I didn't want to force Chris into coming with me in case he wasn't ready. And I wouldn't expect him to be ready. It had barely been 4 months. I would have taken him, I'd told myself that much. I was going to take Chris to the prom, as his boyfriend, if he wanted to go. I just didn't know if he wanted to.

It was Friday night and I knew Zoe was throwing a party tonight. She said she didn't want it to be big, but I knew it would get out of hand and I wanted to be there to help her just in case something happened. But I didn't know what to say to Chris. I know he didn't like being on his own, but I didn't want to leave Zoe and Jake on their own. "Chris?" I asked. We were lying on his bed, my arms were wrapped tightly around him.

"Hmm," he said softly.

"Um, Zoe's having a party tonight," I said, worried what he was going to say. "I...I don't want to leave you but she-"

"Go," he said and I frowned, sitting up and looking at him. I was beyond shocked when I saw he looked slightly angry.

"What's wrong?" I asked, confused. Chris glared at me and sat up.

"Did you think that I'd want to come?" he asked me and my mouth opened but nothing came out. "Of course you didn't. You think I don't want to do anything fun anymore. You're just like everyone else. You treat me like something that could break if you say something wrong."

"Chris, I didn't mean to, I-"

"I know you didn't *mean* to," he sneered, climbing off the bed and standing in the middle of the room. I just sat there confused out of my mind, hurt. "But you still do it. You treat me how you think I want to be treated. I don't want to be babied!"

"Chris! Your mum died! I was just trying to help!" I shouted back at him and his glare turned cold and stony. I realized what I'd said and quickly jumped up, moving towards him. He stepped backwards away from me and I stared at him unsure of what I should do.

"Do you think I don't know that? That's all anyone is able to remind me about!" he snapped. "Do you think I don't see you, Zoe and Jake exchanging worried glances when you think I'm not looking? I don't need you worrying about me!"

"I worry because I care about you!" I shouted back but he didn't say anything, just stared back at me, his gaze cold. "Fine," I said angrily. "Fine. You don't want me to care, I won't." With that, I walked out of his room, slamming the door behind me.

I saw Sean was standing at the bottom of the stairs. When he saw me appear he looked uncomfortably at the floor, not knowing what to do. "Justin-" he started. I just walked past him and left the house. I felt tears running down my cheeks but I ignored them. I just continued walking. I went home and straight up to my room. I slammed my bedroom door behind me and then just stood in the middle of my room fuming. I swiped angrily at my cheeks, trying to stop the never-ending stream of tears. How could he say that to me? The last 4 months all I've done is support him. I hadn't meant to make it worse. God, that's the last thing I wanted. He really resented me that much? I really hurt him that much?

Three hours later I found myself at Zoe's house. I didn't know why I'd come here. I didn't feel like going to a party at all. I just wanted to curl in my bed, wishing that Chris was next to me. I walked into the kitchen and grabbed a bottle off the counter. I didn't even look at what it was. As long as it was alcohol, I was happy. I just needed to let loose for a while before I went back to Chris and tried to fix it between us.

I had planned to have a couple of drinks, stay for a while to make sure Zoe and Jake had it covered, and then leave and go back to Chris and try to talk to him. But before I knew it, I was in the living room, dancing to the loud music, drinking way, way too much. "Hey!" someone shouted. I turned to see a short girl with black hair. I didn't reply, just grabbed her and started dancing with her. I still had a bottle in my hand and drank from it every few seconds. I was angry at Chris for not appreciating what I've done for the last few months. That's the only excuse I had for what I was doing...and what I did next. I finished the bottle, ground my hips against the girl's, and then our lips were joined, smashed together in a passionate make-out session. Our bodies were still moving to the music, still grinding against each other. I could see the lights flashing on my eyelids.

I was suddenly pulled away from whoever I was kissing. I didn't get a chance to say anything before I was pulled into the kitchen. Then I felt the stinging slap of a hand on my cheek. I focused my eyes and saw Zoe glaring at me. "What the fuck are you doing?" she asked me angrily.

"What?" I asked defensively.

"What about Chris? Your *boyfriend?*" she hissed and I clenched my hands into fists.

"We had a fight," I said. Even though I wasn't sure what it was, a fight was the closest thing.

"So?" she asked. "That doesn't give you the right to kiss that girl. In fact, you shouldn't even be here if you had a fight. Go make up with Chris!"

"But he's angry with me," I mumbled sadly.

"So go and fix it," she said, shoving me toward the front door which was wide open.

"He's going to hate me...I have to tell him..." I said. God, how could I have done that? I hated myself for doing that.

"Just fix it first," she said and shoved me out the front door.

I took a deep breath and then started walking. Zoe's house wasn't far from mine and Chris' road, only about a half hour walk. I had walked to the party anyway, so I was forced to walk back. My head was spinning slightly, but I knew I had to talk to Chris. Tonight. I had to fix it before tomorrow. I don't know why I thought that, but I picked up my pace anyway.

Chapter 25

I can't believe he'd left. I mean, not that I blamed him. But...he'd really left. And he'd gone to that party; I'd watched him walk in front of my house on his way there. How could he go to a party after what had just happened between us? I'd lain on my bed, my face buried in my pillow, sometimes crying, sometimes just thinking. I don't even know why I'd gone off at him like that. He was the only one who wasn't treating me differently. I just had to get my anger out...I just hadn't wanted him to take it so badly. I hadn't meant to drive him away. *"You don't want me to care, I won't!"* Every time those words echoed in my head, fresh tears seeped out of my eyes and rolled onto my pillow. I didn't want him to stop caring. He was the only person who I actually wanted to care.

There was a timid knock on my door and my heart faltered. "Mum?" I whimpered, sitting up. She always knocked like that. My heart raced as the door opened and I froze when I saw Justin standing in my doorway. I didn't know how to react for a second but then I jumped off my bed and ran over to him and jumped into his arms, wrapping my legs around his waist and hugging him tightly. "I'm sorry, I'm so, so sorry," I murmured into his ear repeatedly. "I didn't mean it. I love you so much. I'm sorry." Justin's arms were tight around my waist, holding me up. I pressed my lips to his neck and kissed all the available skin. "I'm so sorry, I'm sorry. You've helped me so much. I'm sorry."

"Chris, please stop," he whispered and I pulled back and looked down at him. I frowned slightly, my grip loosening. However, his tight grip held me up.

"You're drunk..." I said softly.

"Just a little..." he murmured. "Please stop apologising. I-"

"But Justin, I *am* sorry. You don't understand. I didn't mean to snap...not at you. It's just everyone else and I didn't mean to take it out on you. I'm sorry." I gazed into his eyes, hoping he would forgive me.

"It's okay, Chris," he said and relief washed through me.

"Really? I mean, I-"

"Chris, I promise you," he said, a slight frown between his eyebrows. "It's okay. You don't need to apologise. I know all this is hard for you. I know you're trying to cope with a lot. And if I'm not there for you to let it out on, who else is going to be there?" I smiled at him and pressed my lips against his. I could taste the alcohol and realized he'd drank more than I had previously thought. I dropped my legs from around him, but he didn't let me go.

"Justin..." I whispered, waiting for his grip to loosen.

"I just want to hold you for a while..." he whispered as he leant on my shoulder. I smiled weakly as tears gathered in my eyes.

"It's okay, I wasn't going anywhere, I was just going to shut the door," I said. He didn't raise his head as he kicked backwards, shutting the door firmly. I smiled slightly and rested my head on his chest. He suddenly picked me up, making me gasp, and then walked over to the bed. He laid me down and then lay on top of me, not letting go of me once. I raised my hand and stroked his hair softly.

"I love you," he breathed in my ear and I smiled. "I care about you...so I'm always going to worry about you." I smiled wider, wrapping my arms around his neck tightly.

"I know," I whispered. "I wouldn't have it any other way."

Justin pulled back so he was a couple of inches above me. He looked down into my eyes and I frowned slightly. Something was wrong. "Chris...I..." he bit his lip and took his eyes away from me. I raised my hand and pulled his chin back to look into his eyes. He gazed into my eyes for what felt like hours. "I...I..."

"What is it, baby?" I whispered. Justin looked down into my eyes and then a small smiled tugged at the corner of his lips.

"I want to go to prom," he said and I frowned. "And I want you to be my date." I stared at him in shock.

"Justin..." I whispered. "Everyone will see...everyone will know..."
"I know," he said, whispering. "I want them to." I stared at him. I knew from his eyes that he did want this. A smile broke out over my face.

"I love you," I said softly.

"I love you, too," he said just as softly.

"Justin..." I started and he smiled in response, waiting for me to continue.

"Make love to me..." Justin's lips opened slightly in shock. We hadn't done anything more than kiss in months. And I don't think it was only me that wasn't ready. It was Justin as well. He hadn't wanted to force me to do anything.

"Really?" he whispered and I nodded.

I stretched up and pressed my lips to his softly, running my hands down his back until I reached the hem of his shirt. I tugged it gently, until Justin's skin was revealed at his lower back. I ran my fingertips along it and felt Justin shiver slightly. His lips skimmed across my jaw and attached to my neck, kissing and nipping at my skin. I moaned softly and moved my hands up Justin's back under his shirt. Soon I could no longer pull it any higher so Justin pulled away and I pulled the shirt over his head. As soon as it was out of the way Justin lowered himself back on top of me and started kissing me again. I felt Justin's hands pulling at my shirt and I arched my back to help him pull it higher. Our kiss broke for a second while he pulled it over my head. Justin then moved lower and pressed kisses down my chest and stomach. My hands went to his hair and knotted in the silky strands. "Justin...please," I whispered. Justin looked up and met my gaze. He continued to look into my eyes as his hands went to my jeans and he unbuttoned and unzipped. He then pulled them off in one fluid motion. I saw Justin smirk.

"No underwear?" he asked and I shrugged.

"You complaining?" I asked and he grinned and leant up and kissed me. I felt his hand stroke my hip teasingly gently. I whined in the back of my throat and Justin grinned. My hands moved to Justin's hips, desperate to rid him of his last items of clothing.

I gasped when Justin's naked body finally pressed against mine. It felt like years since I'd felt him when it had only been a couple of months. "Justin, I need you..." I whispered, lifting my hips to meet his. His hands moved lower and then one finger gently pushed inside of me. I moaned, my back arching off the bed. "More," I whispered. Justin pushed a second finger into me and I moaned louder. I hurt slightly, but I soon got used to it and started pushing my hips onto Justin's fingers. "Jus...I need...I..."

"I know," he whispered, kissing my neck, nipping at the skin. He then removed his fingers and I felt him line himself up with my hole. I closed my eyes, anticipating the feel of having him inside me for the third time. He slowly pushed forward and a moan grew at the back of my throat. I heard Justin moaned as well and then he was kissing my lips passionately, thrusting his tongue into my mouth. Once he was completely inside of me he stayed still. I held back from moving my hips for as long as I could and just enjoyed his kiss, but eventually, I couldn't hold back. I broke the kiss and rotated my hips.

"Justin, move, please," I begged. I saw Justin grin quickly before he buried his face in his neck. He planted kisses all over my skin before pulling part of the way out of me, and then thrusting back in. I moaned, pressing my hips closer to his. I wrapped my legs around his waist, wanting him as close as possible.

"Fuck, Chris," he gasped into my ear. I knotted my fingers in his hair, holding him tightly, as his speed picked up.

"Oh, God," I gasped as Justin hit my prostate hard. My head fell back as Justin proceeded to hit that spot every time. "Jus...I'm gonna...*fuck.*" Justin knew what I was saying. He wrapped his hand around my cock and pumped me in time to his thrusts. I moaned, feeling my orgasm approaching fast. Two more thrusts and I felt Justin swell inside of me and he moaned my name as he came inside of me. The feeling, as well as Justin's hand on my cock, triggered my own orgasm and I came over our stomachs and chests.

Justin then fell over me heavily. But I didn't care. I wrapped my arms around his body, holding him tightly. "I love you," he breathed in my ear, sending shivers down my spine.

"I love you, too," I whispered back. I felt Justin smile against my neck. He shifted slightly, but I wasn't letting go, so he gave up. He sighed contently and I smiled as I closed my eyes. Within seconds, I was asleep.

Chapter 26

-Justin-

I woke up the next morning and saw that Chris was still asleep. I smiled softly at his peaceful face. I wasn't going to do anything to ruin his peace. Even if it meant keeping what happened at the party last night from him. It was a mistake, one I was never going to repeat, and so Chris didn't need to know about it. It wasn't going to affect him, and if I told him, it would just ruin everything. So I was going to keep it to myself. And there was no one who would tell Chris, and that girl goes to a different school. So there was no way that Chris could find out. I just had to make sure Zoe knew not to say anything. Not that she would, but just as a precaution.

I didn't go back to sleep, I just lay there watching my beautiful boyfriend. When he shifted slightly, his hair fell into his face, blocking my view. I frowned slightly and lifted my hand and brushed his hair away. He opened his eyes when my fingertip left his skin and he smiled at me.

"Morning," he said and I smiled back.

"Hey," I replied, gazing into his eyes. He closed his eyes again, moving closer to me and snuggling into my chest. I wrapped my arms around him tightly and buried my face into his hair. I felt something bubble in my stomach and bit my lip. Guilt. Guilt was coursing through my system. I didn't deserve Chris. I had to tell him, but I didn't want to ruin what we had together. And I knew now that it was much too late to go back to being friends if something bad did happen between us.

"What's wrong?" he asked, not lifting his head from my chest.

"What? Nothing's wrong," I said, possibly too quickly. I just had to hope he was still too asleep to notice. He pulled away from me and looked up into my eyes doubtfully. He seemed to look into my eyes for hours, looking for something. Eventually, he looked away and nodded.

"Okay," he said and I frowned. He knew I was lying by saying nothing was wrong. But he didn't want to force me to tell him.

"I love you, Chris, so much," I said softly. He smiled and lifted his hand and stroked my cheek gently.

"I know," he whispered. "I love you, too." I smiled softly and kissed his lips tenderly.

"So what are we doing this weekend?" I asked him and he shrugged.

"I don't want to do anything," he said. "Just stay like this." I smiled and held him slightly tighter.

"Whatever you want, baby," I whispered, kissing his temple.

About an hour later we were forced from Chris' bed by our hungry stomachs. We made our way downstairs and into the kitchen. I realized that Sean wasn't here, and I frowned slightly. He was never around much anymore. "Where's your dad?" I asked Chris, who shrugged.

"Dunno," he said. "He's never home anymore. I've hardly talked to him since..." I frowned but nodded. "I guess he finds it too painful to be here, seeing all her things..." I could hear Chris getting sadder with every word he spoke and I moved towards him. He was turned away from me and as soon as his face came into my view my heart skipped a beat seeing tears running down his cheeks.

"Oh, Chris," I whispered, pulling him against me. He didn't cry, not fully, but tears constantly ran down his cheeks. I held him tightly, rubbing my hand up and down his back.

"He hates me," he whispered into my chest.

"What? Why?" I asked, completely shocked and confused.

"I don't know...but he won't look at me anymore...he won't talk to me anymore..." Chris said. His voice was so full of despair and sadness that tears pooled in my own eyes.

"I'm sure he doesn't hate you, baby," I whispered. "But...you look a lot like your mum. Maybe you remind him of her..." Chris sniffed and nodded minimally into my chest.

"Maybe..." he whispered. "Justin, it's like...like I l-lost them b-both..." I bit my lip and squeezed my eyes together, not wanting my tears to fall. I had noticed that Sean wasn't around so much, but I'd not commented before because I wasn't sure.

"I'm so sorry, Chris," I whispered into his hair. Chris finally let out a sob and then started crying properly. "I know it's not the same," I whispered as he calmed down again. "But you've always got me. Always." He smiled weakly and nodded into my chest.

"Do you think he'll ever talk to me again?" he whispered.

"Of course he will," I said, hoping, praying, that I was right. "He just needs time. You have me...he doesn't have anyone to help him."

"I could help him..." he whispered and I smiled at him softly.

"Baby, you're going through the same thing. And he's your dad. He wants to be strong for you, so showing you how upset he really is, won't be what he wants."

"I wish he would...I don't want him to be strong. I just want my dad back," he said and I nodded.

"I know," I whispered as I stroked his hair.

Chapter 27

-Chris-

The rest of the weekend passed slowly. Dad either didn't come home at all, or managed to sneak in when Justin and I were asleep. I wouldn't let Justin leave me, I didn't want to be on my own, and I don't think he minded. In fact, I think he was more than happy to stay attached to me in one way or another.

When we got back to school Monday morning, Zoe and Jake instantly found us in the car park. "Hey, how you two doing?" she asked. I guessed Justin had told her about our fight on Friday night.

"We're good," Justin said immediately and surely. "I apologized for leaving him and we're all sorted out." I saw as Zoe frowned and shook her head slightly as she looked at Justin. Justin shifted slightly and I wondered what the hell was going on. On the plus side, Jake looked just as confused as me. I was about to ask what was going on, when Justin started pulling me inside the building. I looked back over my shoulder to see Jake and Zoe talking in whispers to each other. I frowned.

"What's going on?" I asked Justin finally.

"Nothing," he said and I frowned. He was lying.

I was about to say something but I saw Jared approaching in the distance. I gasped slightly, not sure what I should do. I then realized that Justin had let go of my hand as soon as Jared came into sight. I bit my lip, not wanting to show how I felt. As Jared got nearer I desperately wanted to reach out to hold Justin's hand, but I forced myself not to. Not only would I be showing weakness to Jared, but Justin wouldn't want me to.

Surprisingly, Jared walked passed me, only shoving me slightly and hissing, "fag." It could have been worse. It had been worse in the past. I saw Justin glance at me, making sure I was okay, but I pretended I hadn't noticed.

"I've got English," I said, turning towards him. "I'll see you at lunch, okay?"

"Yeah," he said softly. "Love you." I felt my heart skip a beat in surprise.

"What?" I asked, shocked.

"You heard me," he said. I looked around and realized that no one was nearby – no one could hear. I smiled weakly and nodded.

"I love you, too," I said and then walked away. I glanced back at Justin and saw he had his hands over his eyes as he lowered his head. I paused slightly, seeing how badly he felt. I bit my lip and sighed. Justin looked up then and met my gaze. I smiled weakly and he smiled just as weakly back. 'Love you,' I mouthed and his smile strengthened. I smiled back and then turned and went to my class.

The whole morning a small smile was on my lips. He'd risked telling me he loved me in the school corridor. Someone could have overheard him. The fact that they didn't is irrelevant. He risked it. Maybe he really was serious about taking me to prom. About coming out.

At lunch Zoe, Jake, Justin and I sat around a table as usual. "Um, Chris..." Justin said after a short while. I turned to him and saw how scared he was. I frowned, worried.

"What's wrong?" I asked.

"About...prom..." he said and my face fell. He'd changed his mind. He didn't want to come out. "No..." he said quickly, moving closer to me. "It's not that," he said, reading my mind. I frowned, wondering what he was talking about.

"What then?" I asked, confused.

"Um," he said nervously. "I just think that...if we turn up at prom together...everyone would be shocked..." I frowned, wondering what he was trying to say. "And...that might ruin it... So...um..."

"Justin," I said, trying to get him to say what he was getting at.

"Maybe...I should come out before prom...so people won't make a big deal when we turn up together..." he said and I stared at him. He was willing to come out?

"Seriously?" I whispered and he smiled and nodded.

"I want to be at prom with you...properly. I don't want people staring at us or asking questions..." Tears pricked in my eyes as he spoke.

"I love you," I whispered and he smiled. He reached over and took my hand.

"Aww." I turned and saw Zoe and Jake smiling at us. I smiled back and squeezed Justin's hand. "So, how are you going to do it?" she asked. I turned to Justin and saw him biting his lip. "You could just tell someone and let it spread...or you could tell everyone..." Zoe said. I frowned slightly and turned back to Justin. "Or you could-" Zoe stopped as soon as Justin leaned forward and pressed his lips against mine. I gasped slightly in surprise and Justin deepened the kiss. I got over my initial shock and then kissed back.

Justin pulled back after a while and rested his forehead on mine. "Or...you could just do that..." I heard Zoe say. I smiled softly and pulled away from

Justin. I looked at Zoe, who was grinning, before returning my gaze to Justin.

"I can't believe you just did that," I whispered and he shrugged.

"About time I did, right?" he asked and I smiled. "And besides, it was the easiest way, too." I then became very aware of several people watching us, and several more whispering and pointing at us. "And now they've got a couple of weeks to get used to it," Justin said and I smiled and nodded.

"Aw, you guys are so cute," Zoe said and I smiled at her.

"Thank you," I grinned and she laughed slightly.

We all then got talking about prom and what we were going to do. It was less than 2 weeks away now, and everyone was excited about it. The three of them talked, and I briefly let my eyes wander around the room.

Suddenly, my gaze met Jared's cold, hateful gaze. My eyes locked with his and I couldn't force my eyes away. The hate and anger and disgust in his eyes sent chills down my spine. I shivered slightly and turned away, focusing back on my friends' discussion. "You okay, baby?" Justin asked me, wrapping his arm around my waist. I smiled and moved more into his embrace.

"I'm perfect," I said softly as he kissed my forehead. I smiled at him, but on the inside I was scared. I was scared about what Jared was going to do to us.

Chapter 28

I was aware of everyone pointing at us but I forced myself to ignore them. For Chris. I had done this for us and I didn't regret it at all. I could now hold my boyfriend's hand as we walked down the corridors. I could kiss him whenever I wanted. And I didn't care what other people said. I was happy. Chris was happy. And that was all that mattered. So what if the occasional person shoved me or hissed horrid words at me? I just ignored it, focusing on the positives.

At the end of school, I met Chris by his car. He smiled at me and pecked me on the cheek. He then got into his car and I followed, getting into the passenger's seat. "How are you?" Chris asked me instead of starting the car. I frowned slightly, confused, and turned to him.

"Fine, why?" I asked. Chris shook his head and looked away. Before he could start the car and escape the conversation, I grabbed his chin and turned him to me. "Chris?" I asked softly and he gazed into my eyes. He then looked away from me and around the car, taking in all the students walking passed.

"Can we talk about it later?" he asked me and I nodded slowly, taking my hand away from his skin.

"Promise?" I asked him and the left corner of his mouth raised in a small smile
"Yeah, I promise," he said and then started the car.

The short car journey was quiet, but neither of us was going to say anything. When we got back to Chris' house, I heard him sigh as he turned the car off. I turned to him and frowned. I didn't have to ask, he answered immediately. "My dad's car isn't here," he said and my heart softened. I think, in his heart, Chris is still waiting for the day when will get back from school and his dad will be waiting with open arms. But I knew that wasn't going to happen, at least, not genuinely. Sean had grown too far apart from Chris to revert back to how he used to behave. I didn't know what to say in response to Chris' statement, but he didn't wait for an answer. He just climbed out the car and then headed for his front door. I watched him for a second and then quickly followed.

I walked through the front door only seconds after Chris, but he'd already moved out of my view. "Chris?" I called out and he appeared in the kitchen doorway. I smiled and followed him. I saw him leaning against the counter, his legs out straight in front of him, his hands on the counter at his sides. I walked over to him and stood in front of him, millimeters from his body. "Talk to me, Chris," I whispered, lifting my hand and gently stroking it down his cheek.

"I'm scared," he whispered and I felt my heart falter in my chest.

"What? Why?" I asked, worry rushing through my system.

"I'm scared for you," he whispered and then confusion clouded my thoughts.

"Me?" I asked, frowning and he nodded. He reached forward, put his arms around my hips and pulled me close to him, my body fully pressed against mine. He buried his face in my shoulder and I felt his breath against my skin.

"I'm used to...how people treat me," he whispered, still hidden in my shoulder. "But...you aren't. Justin, you don't know the half of what's happened to me. And I don't want it to happen to you, too. I...I don't..."He trailed off, holding me tighter.

"What? You don't what?" I asked, my voice soft.

"I don't want to lose you," he whispered and I couldn't speak I was so shocked. Luckily, Chris continued. "If it gets so bad, you might decide I'm...not...worth it." The last few words he said so quietly that I wouldn't have heard him if I hadn't been straining my ears to hear him.

"Chris! How could you think that?" I asked and I felt tears pool in my eyes. "I love you. So much. You are worth everything that people throw at me. I did this for you, so I could be with you. I'm not going to hide or change my mind. I'm with you now, for good." Chris slowly raised his head and looked into my eyes, searchingly, trying to figure out if I was telling the truth or not. Finally, he smiled at me.

"I love you, too," he said and kissed me lovingly.

Chapter 29

-Chris-

Over the next week, as far as I knew, nothing major had happened to Justin as a result of him coming out. And I couldn't express how relieved I was that he had avoided the torture I had endured when I had first come out. I was quite surprised that Jared hadn't done anything to either of us yet. Even me, Jared hadn't even come near me since. Of course, I was happy, but inside, I was still scared. It didn't make sense why Jared had suddenly backed off. I mean, neither Justin nor I were very strong, and he was on the football team. It's not like the odds were against him even with both of us.

Zoe had taken both Justin and I shopping, separately, to buy our tuxes for the prom. We had agreed that we wouldn't see each other's tux until the night. As the days slowly passed, I was getting more and more nervous. I wanted this to go so well, I had the ideal fantasy in my head of how the evening will go. But I didn't want to get my hopes up. I couldn't believe that this night was going to be as incredible as all my imaginings, because if it was anything less, I knew I'd be disappointed. So, I pretended to have very few expectations for the evening. But, inside, I couldn't get rid of the hope that this was going to be one of the bed nights of my life.

The week before prom passed slowly, agonizingly slowly. All I wanted was for it to be Saturday. Even though a part of me was anxious, a larger part couldn't wait for it. I couldn't wait to go to the school prom with Justin as my boyfriend. I couldn't wait to dance with him. I could wait to see him in his tux.

The Friday night before the prom, Justin stayed over at mine. This wasn't anything unusual, as he spent most of his time with me anyway. However, the thing that was unusual was that he went home at about 2 to get ready. I didn't like not being with him, but I knew I would be seeing him again in a couple of hours.

At about 3 o'clock I had a long, hot shower, trying to relax myself. I could already feel myself getting nervous. I spent a long time cleansing my body and washing my hair, just spending as much time as possible under the almost scolding water. Eventually, I stepped out of the shower and walked back into my bedroom. I glanced at the black suit bag hanging on my wardrobe door and took a deep breath. I pulled on a pair of black boxers and a white undershirt and then turned to look in my mirror and started trying to fix my hair. I decided to blow dry it to get it dryer faster, and the applied products to get it to lie exactly as I wanted.

Once I'd finished with my hair I glanced in the mirror and saw it was 4.45. Justin was picking me up at 7.30, so I still had a couple of hours to kill. I looked at myself in the mirror critically. I looked at myself with my glasses on and then took them off and tried to compare the image. I didn't know which looked better. If I didn't wear my glasses, I would have to wear my contacts, which would be a hassle, but then again, I always wear glasses, so maybe not wearing them would be a nice change in celebration of this night? I decided to send a text to Zoe, asking her opinion. **Glasses or no glasses? X** I sent and then went back to trying to make myself look as decent as I could. It was only a few minutes later when I got a reply from Zoe, **Jake said glasses, I say no glasses. So it's up to you. :). X** I rolled my eyes at the lack of help she was.

I finally decided against wearing glasses and went back into the bathroom, which was still steamy and smelt of my shampoo, and tried to put my contacts in. I hated putting them in, hence why I don't wear them very often, but I forced myself to do it this time. Once I had them in, I stared at myself in the mirror again, and sighed and nodded. It would have to do. I went back into my bedroom and sat on my bed and looked at my suit which was hidden inside the garment bag.

About 2 hours later, I was ready. I had my tux on, my electric blue tie lying exactly how I wanted it on the black shirt. My shoes were laced. I was ready to go. But I still had half an hour. Justin was coming to pick me up. I don't know why, but he had insisted that he drive. He'd even managed to talk his mum into letting him borrow her car.

Every few minutes I would straighten my jacket, despite knowing that it didn't matter right now if it wasn't straight. After nearly 25 minutes I heard the doorbell ring and I gasped in surprise. I glanced out of my window and saw Justin's mum's car parked at the end of my drive. I smiled and then turned off my bedroom light as I practically ran down the stairs. I opened the door and felt my breath catch in my throat. While my tux was black, Justin's tux was a dark, midnight blue and he had a grey shirt on underneath with a dark grey tie. He looked incredible; the blue of the suit mixed with the grey of his shirt and tie, really made his blue eyes stand out and I couldn't seem to look away. "Chris...you look..." he whispered and I smiled slightly and blushed.

"Thanks," I said softly. "You, too." He smiled and leaned forward and kissed my cheek tenderly.

"Here," he said and then produced a white rose from behind his back. I felt my heart melt slightly. He reached forward and attached it to my jacket. I looked down at it for a second and then back up into his eyes.

"Come on, baby," he said softly. "Let's go to prom." I smiled and stepped out of door, my hand instantly taking hold of his, as we walked to his car.

Chapter 30

I had never seen anything so beautiful as Chris in a tux. Of course, Chris looked gorgeous in sweats and a hoodie, but in a tux...damn, he looked good. I held his hand as we walked to my car and I opened the door for him. He smiled softly at me in thanks before climbing in. The short drive to school was silent. I think both of us wanted to talk, but we were too anxious about what was going to happen when we got to the school.

About 15 minutes later I pulled into a car park space and stopped the car. There were students everywhere, eager to get inside. I turned to Chris and saw him biting his lip. "You okay, baby?" I asked him softly, reaching over and taking his hand in mine. He smiled slightly and nodded.

"Yeah," he breathed and leant over and pecked my cheek. "Ready?" he asked me and I grinned.

"Always," I said and then we got out of the car. Once our doors were shut I locked the car, if it got stolen my mum would freak. I then walked around and the car and took Chris' hand tightly. I smiled at him and then we started walking towards the school.

We walked through the doors and both froze in awe. The room was dark with colourful lights flashing in the corners and on the ceiling. There was confetti flying around and silver balloons tied to any available space. The music was loud, but not deafening. I turned to look at Chris and saw he had tears in his eyes. "Chris! What's wrong?" I asked, worried. He turned to me and smiled.

"It's perfect," he whispered and I smiled, my heart rate going back to normal.

"Want to dance?" I asked and he grinned and nodded. I squeezed his hand once before pulling him to the dance floor, which was full of other couples as well. It was a fast song, so moved my hands to Chris' hips as we moved together.

It was, without a doubt, one of the best evenings of my life. Everything was perfect. No one had said anything because Chris and I were here together and I knew I'd made the right choice by coming out before prom.

Another reason why I was enjoying this so much was the look of absolute pleasure on Chris' face. I knew that he'd imagined the best prom, and I think this was living up to his dreams. We finally took a break from dancing and moved to get some drinks. Chris had a constant smile on his face and I knew it wouldn't fade anytime soon. "Hey," a voice said behind us and we both turned and smiled at Jake and Zoe. Zoe looked gorgeous in a floor-length black dress with a wide, white belt and a white rose. Jake was wearing a black tux similar to Chris', but he had a white shirt and black tie.

"Hey," Chris grinned and Zoe grinned back at seeing his smile.

"Having a good time?" she asked and Chris nodded happily.

"The best," he said happily. "You?"

"Incredible," Zoe said as she gazed at Jake. I smiled at the couple and then they said bye and walked away.

It was then that a slower song came on and Chris turned to me, his eyes bright. "I love this song, you have to dance with me!" he said and I laughed.

"Like I would say no," I grinned as he pretty much skipped over to the dance floor. My smile couldn't get any wider as I wrapped my arms around his waist and he hooked his arms around my neck. I held Chris as close as possible to me, never wanting to let him go. "I love you," I whispered into his ear and his arms tightened around me.

"I love you, too," he whispered back and I shivered slightly. I felt him smile against my neck and I smiled as well.

We danced slowly, lost in our own little world where only we existed. However, the music suddenly stopped halfway through a song and we pulled back from each other. I glanced around and saw everyone was looking at something. I frowned and followed the direction they were looking and I gasped. "No..." I whispered. At the front of the hall, Jared was standing next to a projector screen. On the screen was a photo, taken just over 2 weeks ago. "No..." I said again and spun around. My eyes met Chris' and I felt my heart twinge. Tears were already coursing down his cheeks. "Chris," I choked out, reaching for him but he took a step backwards, his eyes still on mine. I hated the look he was giving me. It wasn't angry. It was hurt. He was looking at me with so much confusion in his gaze that tears gathered in my eyes. "Chris," I tried again but Chris finally lowered his gaze and stared at the floor. Oh, God. I knew as every second passed I was losing him. "Chris, I-" I stopped talking when Chris turned and walked away from me. I felt my heart shatter. "No! Chris!" I cried but he was already through the door and my feet didn't seem to want to follow what my brain was ordering them.

I turned and glared at Jared, who was smiling smugly at me. This time, my feet did as ordered and I moved forward towards Jared. I wasn't really aware of what I was doing, it was just instinct. I went straight up to him and hit him as hard as I could in the jaw. He didn't go down but when he turned back to me and started to say something, I just hit him again. I didn't give him a chance to defend himself as I hit him over and over again. Soon, I felt someone's hands on me, pulling me back. "Justin! Justin, stop!" It was Jake shouting, it was his hands pulling me away.

"Justin! This isn't helping anything. Go find Chris!" It was Zoe this time. I registered what she said and quickly turned away and ran out of the hall.

Chapter 31

-Chris-

I couldn't get the image out of my head. Justin had his tongue thrust down some random girl's throat and I don't think they could have gotten any closer to each other. But the one thing on the picture that stuck out in my head was the date stamped in orange in the bottom right corner of the photo. Two weeks ago. It was when we'd had our fight and Justin had gone to Zoe's party. He'd hooked up with a girl while I'd been at home crying. Why didn't he tell me? When he'd come back to me later that evening. That night was marked in my mind because it was the first time we had been...together since mum had passed away. Now it was marked as something else. It was when Justin had started lying to me. I should have known something was wrong, but being the naive person I am, I just assumed he was upset because we'd had a fight.

I continued walking home. I felt my phone vibrating in my pocket but I ignored it. I didn't want to talk to anyone right now. I knew that as soon as I got home Justin would come looking for me. So I quickly changed my direction. I tried to stay off the roads Justin would use to drive home and slowly walked towards the church. It took me about half an hour to walk there but one I did I opened the black metal gate and walked into the graveyard. Going to a graveyard at night probably isn't the most sensible thing to do, but I didn't care. I didn't want to go home. I walked straight through the graves, my feet instinctively knowing where I was going. When my eyes landed on the grave I was headed towards I felt my knees give out and I fell to the floor. Despite this, I crawled over to my mum's grave and knelt in front of it, gazing at the stone that represented my mum. Tears trickled down my cheeks.

"I miss you," I whispered to the stone, wishing that I could be speaking to mum again. "I need you so much. I don't know what to do. You always knew what to do. I wish you could help me." I paused as I thought about Justin again. "I didn't think we'd be over so quickly. We only lasted 4 months. That's it. I thought that we'd be together forever. I loved him so much and I thought he loved me... How could he do that to me? None of this is fair. I wish I could go back in time and be stronger, not let Justin get to me, not fall in love with him. If I hadn't fallen for him then we'd still be friends now and it would be so much easier." I paused for a second as I thought and then I sighed. "Actually, I don't wish that. I don't regret being with Justin, and I don't wish it had never happened. I just wish it had lasted a bit longer. I guess I experienced true happiness for a short time, and now it's over. Why do some people get a happily ever after and some don't? It's not fair. Maybe I don't deserve a happy ending. Maybe I deserve to have Justin break my heart. Maybe I deserve this pain." I ran my hand over the stone smoothly. "I wish you could help me, mum. You would know what I should do."

I then leaned against the stone and looked up into the sky. It was a clear night and I hoped it stayed that way. I wasn't going home so I prayed it wasn't going to rain. I felt safe sitting here with my mum and slowly my eyes began to shut and I fell asleep.

"Hey, kid?" I heard and I frowned as I opened my eyes. I came face to face with an old man who was gazing down at me, concern etched in the deep wrinkles on his face. "You okay?" he asked. I realized that I must look a hell of a sight. Seventeen year old boy, in a black tux, probably with tear tracks on my cheeks, sleeping against a grave. "Kid?" he asked again and I looked up at him. "Do you need any help?" he asked and I shook my head.

"I'm okay," I said, my voice sounding weak.

"Do you want me to call anyone?" he asked and I shook my head again.

"I'm okay," I repeated, my voice starting to come back. I stood up and looked back down at my mum's grave. "I love you," I whispered and then walked out of the graveyard and headed home.

The walk home took nearly an hour, but I didn't care. I was in no hurry. I had to also change my path to avoid walking passed Justin's house. But eventually I got home and went straight up to my room. I went and sat on my bed, but then all the memories of when Justin and I had been together on my bed came back to me and I jumped off it. I shivered, wondering if, when he'd been with me, he'd also been with someone else as well. Tears pricked in my eyes. I suddenly felt really dirty and took my tux off and went into my bathroom. I turned my shower on as hot as it goes and stepped under the scalding spray. I hissed at the boiling water hit my skin, but I didn't make it colder. The pain felt good.

About an hour later I got dressed in sweats and a hoodie and went downstairs into the kitchen. I stood there for a second and then I went into dad's study. "Hey, dad," I said softly and dad looked up from his computer.

"Hey, Chris," he smiled softly. I felt tears pricking in my eyes and I quickly crossed the room and hugged him tightly. Dad was slightly surprised but hugged me back anyway. Tears trickled silently from my eyes as I buried my face in his chest. "Chris? What's wrong?" he asked, pulling me away from him and looking into my watery eyes.

"I miss mum," I choked. I wasn't lying either, I just told him part of it. I saw my dad's face soften and he pulled me back against him.

"I know, I miss her, too," he murmured. "Chris, I've been thinking," he said and I could sense the seriousness in his tone and pulled back. "I was thinking that we should make a fresh start. I can't help but think about her when we're here. Of course, I don't want to forget about her, but I just think it would be easier to move on if we...moved." My eyes widened somewhat as I stared at him.

"You mean...go to a new town?" I asked and dad nodded.

"And I know you will miss-"

"That's fine," I said immediately and dad frowned in shock.

"What?" he asked.

"That's fine," I repeated. "I want to move, too. Fresh start, right?"

"Chris, what-"

"Where should we go?" I asked, interrupting his question because I already knew what it would be.

"I was actually looking at Southampton," he said and I quickly thought.

"Sounds great," I grinned and dad frowned even more.

"Chris, just listen for a second," he said and I bit my lip. "Why are you so enthusiastic to move?"

"I want a fresh start too," I said. "Meet new people, make new friends. Meet someone...who...might..." I couldn't help it as new tears spilled from my eyes. Dad took me back into his arms and wrapped his arms around me tightly.

"What happened, Chris?" he asked and I took a deep, shaky breath.

"H-He cheated on me," I whispered and I felt dad tense slightly.

"What!?" he almost shouted but I shook my head.

"It doesn't matter," I muttered. "It's over now, and I can have a fresh start."

"Chris, are you sure-"

"Absolutely," I said and stood up. "The sooner I'm away from here, the better."

Chapter 32

-Justin-

He wasn't answering my calls, which didn't really surprise me. "Just give him time," Zoe said and I sighed and nodded. I guess there was nothing else I *could* do. Just give him time. I just had to pray that after I had given him time, he would hear me out. If I lost Chris for good, I don't know what I'd do. I needed him and I wasn't going to let Jared ruin it.

Chris didn't come to school. For the first week I want really worried. I mean, to be honest, he'd been humiliated in front of the whole school. But once the time period stretched to a month, I started to worry. It wasn't like Chris to miss that much school. What if something had happened? I knew I should have just forced him to let me talk to him. I didn't care if it made it any worse, because it couldn't really get any worse. I just had to tell him the truth, explain it to him properly. Because he didn't know the truth. He probably thought I'd been doing shit like that the whole time we'd been together.

So I decided that enough was enough. I'd given him a month to come round but nothing. So I decided I would go see him. As soon as school was out, I jumped into the car my parents were lending me seeing as Chris no longer gave me a lift to school, and drove straight to Chris' house. I slammed on the breaks when I saw a sign outside Chris' house. Luckily there was no one else around but I didn't care. I just stared at the small sign on top of a post in Chris' front garden. It was dark blue with a company's name written on top in white. But all I cared about was the large 'SOLD' written in white on a red background. I looked into the house and saw through the windows that all rooms were empty. They were gone? How could he leave? Tears ran down my cheeks. Oh, God.

I drove the short distance home and then ran inside. "Justin?" mum called but I ignored her. "Justin, you have post." I frowned, confused, and wiped my tears away. I rarely got post. I walked into the kitchen and she passed me a letter. I saw she was about to ask me why I was crying to I quickly retreated up to my room. I recognized the writing on the front of the envelope immediately and my stomach tightened. Maybe he would tell me where he's gone. Maybe he would give me an address. Maybe he would tell me that he didn't want to, but his dad made him leave. Maybe he would tell me he loves me. Maybe he would tell me he already misses me. I bit my lip in anticipation as I peeled the envelope open. My heart was racing as I pulled out the folded piece of paper. I took a deep breath and then opened it. And my heart faltered. Two words. That's it. That's all I got. ***Goodbye, Justin.***

I fell to the floor, gripping the letter and cried. He'd really gone. He'd left me. What was I going to do now? How could I go on without him? He was my life. I should have explained everything when I had the chance instead of giving him time. All I did was give him time to escape. I curled into a ball, still holding the letter tight. No, no, no. How could this have happened? Everything was so perfect and I had to go and fuck it up. I can't believe I let him leave me. There was a knock on my door but I didn't react to it. But it opened anyway. Two sets of footsteps entered the room. Someone sat next to me and I opened my eyes long enough to see it was Zoe. I sat up and flung my arms around her. "He's gone," I cried and she held me tightly. "He's gone." I kept repeating it as Zoe tried her hardest to comfort me. But nothing anyone did could help me. The only person who could help me was gone. I was never going to see him again.

Chapter 33

-Chris-

Fresh start. New people. New friends.

Yeah right.

No one wanted to be friends with a depressed 18 year old. And I didn't blame them. I wouldn't want to be friends with me. I must have been insane to believe that moving an hour away would help me to forget about Justin. Nothing could, nothing ever would. But this place seemed to be working for my dad. He hadn't forgotten about mum, he'd just started moving on. He still went to visit her grave once a month, but he was back to his old self. He made new friends quickly, compared to me, and seemed to be simply happier.

The months had passed slowly. I hadn't finished the school year, so I hadn't graduated, but I didn't really care. I got a job at a small newspaper where one of my dad's new friends worked. It was nothing important, but it was a good experience and I hoped that, over time, I would be able to do something more. I put all my energy into working there and trying to impress the right people.

Dad tried to introduce me to some people my own age. He even introduced me to sons of his new friends, who he thought I would be interested. But no matter what the guys were like, my response was always the same, "I'm not looking for a relationship." Because I wasn't. I wasn't going to be with anyone else. The one person who I would consider spending my life with had stabbed me in the back. I wasn't going to let anyone in.

I missed Justin. I truly did, more than I thought was possible. I wanted to email, phone, write to him, but I couldn't. I wanted to hear his voice, but I was too scared. He would have moved on by now. He would have forgotten about me, found someone new.

I missed Zoe and Jake as well. I wanted to keep in contact with them, but I was scared that, if I did, then Justin would find out where I was and try to contact me. And I don't think I could handle him contacting me.

Soon, nearly 7 months had passed since we'd moved and my mind kept reminding me of the date. It was a year ago on Friday that Justin had told me he loved me in the middle of the park in the rain. I couldn't help but smile at that memory. Before everything had gone downhill. On Thursday night I couldn't sleep. The whole memory kept running through my head, not letting me relax. At 5 o'clock I sighed and threw off my blankets. I went and had a long, hot shower, trying to relax my body. It didn't work. I got out the shower just as tense as I had been before. I sighed and went back to my bedroom.

I liked this house. True, it wasn't exactly *home* but...there were no memories in this house. A fresh start. There was nothing in this house that I would see and would suddenly get upset. This house was slightly smaller than our old one, but neither of us really cared.

After I'd got dressed in sweats and a t-shirt I went downstairs in the dark. The sun would be rising in about an hour. I went through to the kitchen and made myself a cup of coffee. I didn't know what to do. My brain was telling me to do something, but I was adamantly ignoring it.

I spent most of the day doing odd jobs that needed to be done, but there was no urgency to. I did some bits of laundry, cleaned some dishes, hoovered an already clean floor. My dad kept watching me, frowning slightly but I pretended I didn't see.

By 3 o'clock I couldn't stand it anymore. "I'm going out," I said and he nodded. "I...I don't know if I'll be back tonight. I'll phone you, okay?"

"Where are you going?" he asked and I hesitated.

"Just...for a drive," I said and he looked at me for a second. Then something seemed to click and he smiled softly and nodded.

"Okay, be safe," he said and I nodded and ran up to my room. I quickly got changed into a pair of jeans and pulled on a hoodie before going back downstairs. I grabbed my phone and my keys and then went outside and got into my car.

The drive was long, but only because I didn't it reasonably slowly. I was kind of hesitant about this whole thing. I didn't know what was going to happen and I didn't like that. Eventually I started driving through familiar roads and I couldn't help the smile that appeared on my lips. I had missed this place. As soon as I thought that, a drop of water hit my windscreen. And then, as though that was their cue, hundreds of other drops fell from the sky. I smiled humourlessly. *It was raining then, and it's raining now,* I thought.

It was starting to get dark by the time I parked in the car park, but it was still reasonably early and many people were still around. I got out of my car and sat on the bonnet and watched people walk into and out of the park. Soon, most of the people were leaving the park. I looked at my watch and saw it was nearly 8.30. I frowned as I wondered how I had managed to sit here for that long. I slid off my car and slowly made my way into the park. I walked hesitantly, still unsure if I should be here at all. I wondered if Justin knew what today was. I wondered if he cared.

I walked, hands in my pockets, under the trees, getting further into the darkness. I remembered how I had felt this time last year. I was heartbroken because I thought Justin didn't love me. I just wanted to be miserable. I sighed and continued walking. I rounded a corner and froze as my eyes landed on a figure. That couldn't be... Sitting on the bench, hunched over in the rain and shaking was... "Justin?" I whispered, tears in my eyes. He didn't hear; he was too far away. But I knew it was him. Now I was stuck. I didn't know whether I should just turn around and leave or if I should go over to him.

While I was still contemplating, my feet started moving. I was getting nearer and nearer to Justin. He didn't move as I approached him and I figured he hadn't realized I was there. "Justin?" I whispered.

"What are you doing here?" he asked. Déjà vu. Except we'd swapped places and lines. I hated how he sounded. His voice was flat, void of emotion. He wanted me to believe that he didn't care, but I could see the tears.

"Same thing as you," I said, sitting next to him on the bench.

"Remembering." He raised his head and finally looked at me and I gasped slightly. The pain in his eyes made my heart twinge painfully in my chest. He quickly looked away again and I saw him screw his eyes closed tight. I wanted to say something, anything, but I didn't know what. Suddenly there was a flash, followed by the growl of thunder. In that instant, my world changed. Justin's wrists. In the light given in that split second, silvery scars had been illuminated on his skin. As well as light pink scars...fresh scars.

"No...Justin..." I whispered. He didn't respond. I reached over and took his arm in my hands gently. I pulled up his sleeve and as I did so, Justin turned his head away, as though disgusted. I ran my fingers down his arm softly, feeling the ridges under my fingertips. "Justin," I whispered, taking my eyes away from the scars and back to his face, but he wouldn't look at me. I frowned and raised my hand to his chin and turned his head back to me. "Why?" I whispered, tears in my eyes. He looked up and met my eyes and felt my breath catch in my throat.

"I hate myself," he whispered and felt my heart skip a beat. I could tell by his tone and the look in his eyes that he meant exactly what he said. I thanked whoever was out there that Justin hadn't gone any further than cutting...that Justin was still here. I moved my hand slightly until it was tightly holding his. Neither of us said anything more, we just sat in the rain holding hands.

I don't know how much time passed before Justin made a small noise. I quickly turned to him and saw he was now sobbing into his free hand. Tears instantly gathered in my eyes but I didn't know what to say. He pulled his hand out of mine and shifted away from me slightly. "I never deserved you, Chris," he whispered after a while and my heart softened. "You were always too good to me. I didn't deserve someone like you. I never loved you in the way you deserved to be loved and I hate that I couldn't give you what you deserve. But the thing is...now I've had you, even for a short while, I can't forget about you, I can't get over you. I'll never be able to stop loving you. And I know you probably moved on, there's no reason why you wouldn't. But I want you to know I'm sorry. I'm so, so sorry. I never meant to hurt you. That...that picture...was...a mistake. I n-never meant t-to...I...I was drunk and..." He stopped and hung his head. "It doesn't even matter now, does it?" he asked bitterly and I knew he wasn't expecting a response. "It's all in the past, and yet it's still with us now. I can't forget about it because I regret losing you each and every day. I can't stop loving you, and you will probably never stop hating me." I opened my mouth but nothing seemed to come out. I was amazed at how much being close to Justin, hearing Justin speak, reminded me just how much I loved him. "I am sorry, Chris," he whispered. My eyes widened as he stood up without another word and started walking away. I sat in confusion for a couple of seconds, long enough for him to get quite a distance away. But I suddenly snapped out of it and realized that my one chance for happiness was slowly walking away from me.

"Justin," I whispered but he was too far away to hear me. I quickly stood up and started running after him. "Justin!" I called when I was near enough. He turned just in time for me to run straight into him, wrapping my arms around his neck, and throwing both of us to the floor. I heard him gasp, but then my mouth covered his as I kissed him passionately. My hands knotted in his rain-soaked hair and his pulled at my drenched hoodie. We both wanted to get as close as we possibly could to one another after being alone for so many months. However, eventually, we both had to breathe. I pulled away and looked down at him, both of us breathing heavily. I moved my head so that no rain landed on Justin's face and gazed down into his eyes. "Justin, do you really need me to say it?" I asked, a small smile on my lips as I repeated words he'd said to me last time we were in the park in the rain. I saw Justin's lips part in shock but he didn't say anything. I smiled softly and leaned down so my lips were next to his ear. "I love you. I always will." I heard him gasp slightly and then he pushed me off onto my back and rolled on top of me and gazed down at me. I could feel the mud seeping into my clothes but I didn't care. We gazed into each other's eyes for what felt like an eternity as the storm worsened around us.

"Seriously?" he whispered and I smiled.

"I seriously love you," I whispered, raising my hand to the back of his neck.

"I seriously love you, too," he whispered, resting his forehead on mine.

"And I'm never letting you go again," he said, gripping my shirt tight.

"Never, never, never." I grinned and wrapped my arms around his shoulders.

"Good," I said and leaned up and kissed him deeply.

Chapter 34

I couldn't believe he'd come back. I couldn't believe that he'd come back to the park. I thought for sure that he would have moved on, that he wouldn't remember what the day was. And yet here he was, in my arms, after all these months. And he'd forgiven me. That was the most miraculous thing about it all. I didn't think I would ever be able to let him go, I didn't want the contact to end, I needed to hold him to ensure that he was really here and that I wasn't imagining it. I continued to gaze down at him. I could feel the rain pummelling against my back but I didn't care, not one bit. "Justin, we need to get out of the rain," Chris said after a while, trying to move, but I shook my head, whimpering and clinging on tightly. I saw Chris was slightly shocked by my reaction, and so tightened his arms back around me. "Justin, I'm not going to leave," he whispered into my ear. I just shook my head.

"D-Don't want to let you go," I murmured as I buried my face in his shoulder. "Not again."

"I know you don't," he said. "I won't let you." I still hesitated before pulling away. I was so scared that if I moved away from him, even slightly, that he would vanish. I gripped his hand tightly, and I'm sure it was hurting him, but I couldn't let him leave me again. I pulled away slowly and pulled him up with me by his hand. "Justin," he said once we were both standing. "I love you. You're not going to lose me. I promise." I gripped his hand tighter, if that was possible. "Come on, my car is in the car park." I nodded and we slowly started walking towards his car. Neither of us said anymore. I don't think either of us knew where to start.

A few minutes later, we were both finally out of the rain, sitting in Chris' car. It hadn't changed at all. I smiled, remembering all the times I'd spent in his car. "I'll take you home," he said and I turned to him.

"You're staying with me, right?" I asked and he looked at me. He only barely hesitated before nodding. That barest hesitation still brought tears to my eyes and I quickly looked away before he could see.

The car journey back to my house was silent. As soon as Chris pulled up outside my house I turned to him. He glanced at me before getting out of the car. I followed him and we walked into my house together. My parents were probably both asleep by now, so Chris and I were silent as we walked upstairs. Once my bedroom door was shut behind us, I let out a breath. He was still here with me. "Justin," he said softly and I looked into his sad eyes. "I can't come back." I gasped slightly, my heart lurching painfully. He didn't want to come back to me? I lowered my head. It was understandable really. I had cheated on him. Whether I'd done it intentionally or not, it had still happened. I didn't deserve him to forgive me, I didn't deserve him to love me anymore. I felt Chris' fingers on my chin, raising my head so my eyes met his. "Don't think like that," he said, knowing what I was thinking. "It's not because of you. You're the reason I *want* to come back. But...I can't do that to my dad." I frowned slightly, questioning with my eyes. "He's better now. He's...coping better than he was when we were here. He's slowly moving on. And I won't force him to come back to a place where he was suffering. I can't." I frowned slightly as I thought of something.

"You...You moved because of your dad?" I whispered.

"Um, mostly," he said and I nodded. It was reasonable that Chris wouldn't want to be around me. "When dad told me he wanted to move...I just didn't object. I wanted to...run away. I didn't want to have to...face you after what happened." Tears pricked in my eyes but I nodded anyway. He raised his hand again and cupped my jaw, his thumb softly stroking my cheek. "Justin, I didn't ask to leave here because of you. You have no idea how hard being away from you for a year has been..." he whispered and I lowered my eyes, my fingers immediately going to the dozens of scars on my wrists.

"How could you say I have no idea?" I asked, my voice coming out harsher than I had intended. "It killed me that you ran away from me. You have no clue how many times I tried to..." I trailed off, realizing what I had been about to say. But Chris had caught on.

"Tried to what?" he asked, fear in his voice, and I looked away. I brought my arms up and gazed at the hideous scars marring my skin.

"I hate myself, Chris," I whispered, tracing one of the deepest cuts. "I hate what I did. I hate that I hurt you. I hate that I drove you away from me. I hate that I had to live without you. And I just couldn't. I couldn't live without you. I didn't want to. And yet...I could never do it. Not properly." I remembered the time when my parents had found me in the bathroom, blood pouring from my wrists. I knew my mum's scream would haunt me for the rest of my life. I hadn't cared what it had done to my parents. I just couldn't live in a world where I wasn't allowed to be with Chris.

I snapped out of my thoughts when I felt Chris' warm hand close over mine on my wrist. I looked up and gasped slightly when I saw Chris had tears running freely down his cheeks. "I shouldn't have left you," he choked and tears then started falling from my eyes. "I'm so sorry. If...If you had g-gone...I would n-never have f-forgiven myself..." I pulled Chris against me tightly. He cried silently into my shoulder.

"Chris, please don't blame yourself," I whispered. "This is all my fault. But...I have learned something while you've been gone." Chris pulled away and looked up at me, frowning in confusion. "I never loved you right. I never loved you how you deserved to be loved. And I promise you, if you give me another chance, I will give you everything you want. Everything you deserve. I'm not going to lose you again and I'll do anything to show you how much I love you, how much I need you."

"I never wanted anything more than you," Chris whispered and I frowned and shook my head.

"You deserve more than what I gave you," I replied, and this time Chris frowned and shook his head.

"I deserve whatever you're willing to give me," he said softly. "All I want...is for you to love me. There isn't a right way for you to do it. There isn't a perfect way for you to do it. And I'm okay with that. I'm happy with that." I gazed into his eyes and lowered my forehead until it rested on his.

"I love you, Chris," I whispered. "So, so much."

"I love you, too," he whispered back.

Chapter 35

Justin and I both had showers because we knew that we couldn't go to sleep considering how wet, cold and covered in mud we were. I went first, trying to be as quick as possible so Justin could have his shower, while trying to wash completely and warming up. And we had to be as quiet as possible, because it was gone midnight and his parents were asleep. I went back into Justin's room as he had his shower, and got dressed in a pair of Justin's sweats and chose to leave my chest bare. I looked around Justin's bedroom. I hadn't been in here in nearly a year but I realized that it hadn't changed much. I found that reassuring.

A few minutes later Justin walked through his bedroom door and silently shut it behind him. I felt my breath catch in my throat as my eyes landed on him. He was only wearing a towel, tied low around his hips. There were water droplets still running down his body, dripping from his hair. I quickly looked away, at my hands in my lap. I heard Justin getting dressed – pulling on boxers and a t-shirt. He then came and sat next to me on the bed, but I kept my eyes lowered. I watched as Justin's hand moved and took hold of mine tightly. I slowly raised my head and looked into Justin's eyes. I bit my lip before closing the gap between us and kissing him tenderly. I raised my free hand and cupped Justin's jaw. Slowly, the kiss grew more passionate and we both moved closer to each other. My other hand moved away from Justin's hand, and moved up and curled around Justin's neck, while both of his hands went to my hips and pulled me closer to him. Before I even knew what had happened, I was lying over Justin, covering his neck in kisses while running my hands up and down his sides. I quickly pulled the t-shirt off him and moved down and started kissing his chest. "Chris," Justin moaned, pushing at my shoulders. I quickly pulled back, wondering if I'd done something wrong.

"Can...you...um...I mean..." I frowned slightly and cupped his face, bringing his eyes up to meet mine.

"What, baby?" I whispered. My concern grew as I saw tears gather in his eyes. "Justin? What's wrong?" I asked, alarmed.

"Make love to me," he whispered and I gasped softly. Did he mean he...? I gazed down into his eyes and felt tears gather in my own eyes. "I-I want to feel...you. Please," he whispered desperately. Who was I to deny him when he asked me like that? I smiled softly and leaned down and kissed him softly.

"Anything you want, baby," I whispered. I pulled back again and quickly pushed off my sweats and then Justin's boxers quickly followed. I glanced into his eyes as I asked, "have...have you done...this before?"

"No!" he said, almost angrily. "It's only you, Chris. Only you." I smiled softly and pecked him on the lips before moving lower on his body.

"This is going to hurt, tell me if you want me to stop," I said and Justin nodded minutely. I brought my finger to my mouth and sucked it, as that was the only lube we had. Justin stared at me and bit his lip and I smirked slightly. I then lowered my hand and gently pushed into Justin. He gasped but made no attempt to stop me, so I continued. I held my finger still and eventually pulled it back before pushing back in. After a short while, I pushed in a second finger. I could hear Justin's breathing and I held my fingers still for him to get used to. I saw a tear running down his cheek and my heart twisted. I moved up and kissed the tear away. "I can stop," I whispered but he shook his head.

"Please don't," he whispered back and I nodded. I then started moving my fingers in and out and scissored them to stretch him as much as possible, to ensure it would hurt less. After a few minutes, I knew that I couldn't stretch him anymore. I removed my fingers and heard him gasp as I did.

"Are you-" I started.

"Yes! Please, I want to feel you," he gasped, interrupting me. I lined myself up and my face hovered inches above his. I looked into his eyes as I slowly pushed forward. I saw pain in his eyes and I knew how hard he must be trying to keep the eye contact. So I leaned down and kissed him, breaking the eye contact when my eyes closed. I pushed completely inside and then froze, letting Justin get used to it. I had to admit that this felt weird for me. I'd always bottomed, never topped before. It wasn't a bad weird. It just felt different. I could definitely get used to it.

"Are you okay?" I whispered, trying to catch my breath. Justin nodded, breathing hard. I slowly pulled back and then gently pushed back in.

"Chris..." Justin moaned and my head fell and rested on his shoulder. God, I'd missed the way he moaned my name. It was the things I didn't even realize I'd missed that I was suddenly aware of missing. Slowly, my speed increased, but I made sure that Justin was okay with it. The only responses I got to my questions, however, were pleasure filled moans. And then Justin nearly screamed when I hit his spot. I quickly stopped him from screaming, though, by kissing him, because his parents were still only a couple of doors away. "Oh, God, Chris," he gasped and I continued to aim for that same spot. "Fuck..."

"God, Justin," I whispered into his ear. I could feel my orgasm building and I reached between us and moved my hand up and down on Justin's cock in time with my thrusts. Justin moaned in response and I felt his muscles clenching around me, suggesting he was close as well. "I love you so much," I whispered and he moaned and suddenly came hard in my hand. Feeling him clench around me subsequently sent me over the edge as well and we both rode out our orgasms together.

I eventually rolled off Justin and lay on my back, breathing hard. Only a few seconds later, Justin curled into my side. I smiled and wrapped my arms around him after pulling the blanket over us. "I love you, too," he whispered and I grinned and placed a soft kiss on his forehead. We lay there for a while longer, but neither of us fell asleep. I just wanted to stay awake and soak up every second I had with Justin. And I think he was doing the same. "Which do you like better?" he asked after a while and I turned to him.

"What?" I asked and I saw a blush on his cheeks. I didn't remember Justin being this conscious around me before. Or maybe he had been and I just hadn't noticed...

"Bottoming or topping?" he asked and I smiled. I thought about it for a second.

"Bottoming, I think," I told him. "That was incredible but I still think I prefer bottoming. You?"

"Topping," he smiled and I smiled as well. "I-I just...wanted to feel you. I needed you. I had to make sure you really were here." I tightened my arms around him.

"I'm here," I whispered into his ear and I felt his shiver in my arms. "I promise. And nothing is going to separate us again. I'll always be here with you."

"I missed your voice," Justin sighed and it sounded as though he was falling asleep. I glanced down at him, to see his eyes were closed and he was fast asleep. I smiled softly and snuggled into the bed as I pulled him to me tighter. I was already dreading the time when I had to go back to Southampton. I didn't know how I would leave him. I didn't know what he would do when I left. I traced my finger down the scars on his arm as tears started to run down my cheeks.

Chapter 36

I was smiling even before my eyes opened the next morning. I could feel the length of Chris' body alongside mine. "Morning," Chris whispered and I grinned and opened my eyes and looked at him.

"Morning," I said softly. I then realized that his eyes seemed to be really heavy. "Did you not sleep?" He shook his head. "Why not?"

"I was thinking," he said and I frowned.

"About?" I asked softly.

"You..." he whispered sadly and I frowned again. I realized then that he was looking down at my arms and brought my arms behind me so he couldn't see. "Sorry, I...I just..." he said and I nodded. I lowered my head, ashamed. Chris then reached out and tenderly lifted my chin and forced me to look into his eyes. "Justin, please," he whispered and slowly reached for my hand.

"Do...do you hate me...for doing this to myself?" I asked, scared.

"What? No!" he said adamantly. "I...I hate that you did this because of me." I lowered my head.

"I'm sorry," I whispered.

"I know," he whispered, tightening his hold on me. "Promise me you won't do it again."

"I promise," I whispered, my hands gripping his shirt tightly. "Now that I have you, I'll be okay."

"And...And what about when I've gone back?" he asked and I tensed.

"I promise I won't," I whispered, not wanting to think about that time. "I know you'll come back. Right?"

"Of course, Justin," he said immediately. "I'll come back as many times as I can. Nothing would keep me away." I smiled softly and snuggled into his side. "So, what are we doing now?" he asked.

"Nothing," I said, closing my eyes. "Just hold me, please."

"Always," he whispered as he pressed his lips against my forehead and held me against his chest. I smiled and sighed in content.

A few hours later, Chris started talking about him having to get back. I didn't want him to. I really wanted him to stay. But I knew he had to get back, his dad would be wondering where he was. "When will I see you again?" I asked him softly after we'd both gotten dressed. He turned to me, his eyes sad. I knew I wasn't making this easy, but I didn't really care. "Soon," he said and I nodded sadly. That wasn't a proper answer. 'Soon' could really mean anything. Chris came over to me and hugged me tightly. "I should really be with my dad next weekend," he said and I remembered that it was the one year anniversary of his mum's death. I nodded. Chris pulled away from me and went over to my desk and wrote something down. "My new number," he said, handing me the paper. I smiled at him as I took it. He gazed down at me for a while and then sighed. "I really don't want to leave you again," he said and I realized I was making it too hard for him and I felt slightly guilty.

"You're not," I said softly. "At least, not in the same way you did last time.

"We'll see each other again soon."

"I love you, Justin," he whispered and I smiled and kissed him tenderly.

"I love you, too, so much," I whispered back. "We can make this work. I know we can." He smiled and nodded before pressing another kiss to my lips.

A few minutes later, Chris was climbing into his car. I leaned down and kissed him once more through the open window, and then he turned and slowly drove away.

Chapter 37

I hated being back in Southampton. I hated being away from Justin. But I knew I couldn't ask my dad to move back, not so close to the 1 year anniversary of mum's passing. But Justin and I phoned each other numerous times a day. And whenever I could, I went back to see him, and he occasionally borrowed his mum's car and came to Southampton.

But we both knew that it wasn't enough. Both of us were very aware of the fact that we weren't seeing each other as much as we wanted. Whenever we did meet up, I always subtly glanced at Justin's wrists, just to be sure, but there was no sign that he had done anything. I couldn't express my relief that he had stopped hurting himself.

Life carried on, however. I still went to work at the newspaper and saved up money. On my 18th birthday, Justin came down and stayed the weekend. It was an incredible weekend, simply because we hadn't seen each other in a while. But that's not what I will remember that weekend for. The day after my birthday, my dad pulled me aside, telling me he had something to talk to me about. I frowned slightly, but sat in his study with him. "Chris," my dad started. "When...your mum passed away...she..." He paused and I could see how hard it was for him to talk about mum. "Your mum and I made our wills together. And we both set aside money for you, if either or both of us died. And, now that you're 18...you can access that money." I sat there, my mouth slightly open in shock.

"Mum...left me money?" I asked, not really able to grasp it.

"Yes," dad nodded. "It's enough to, if you want, rent your own place. You probably don't want to live with your dad anymore, right? And besides, I thought you might be able to get an apartment...nearer to Justin..." My mouth parted even more as his words completely sunk in. Justin and I...we could...

"Seriously?" I whispered and dad smiled and nodded. A grin suddenly appeared on my face. I jumped up and wrapped my arms around dad in a tight hug. "Thank you, dad." Dad just smiled and nodded and pushed me towards the door. I grinned and didn't hesitate before running out of the room and upstairs to my room, where Justin was waiting.

I burst through the door and ran over to my bed and practically leaped onto Justin, pushing him back onto the bed. He just laughed as his arms went around me and held me. I lifted my head and looked down at him, a ridiculous grin etched on my face. "What?" Justin asked, obviously realizing that something was up. I just grinned and kissed him passionately. I was too happy to explain it to him now. Justin immediately kissed me back. I cupped his face in my hands as we made out, but eventually the intensity of the kiss died down and I pulled away slowly.

"Move in with me?" I asked immediately, not really thinking about what I was saying. Justin frowned at me, clearly confused.

"What?" he asked.

"I'm going to get an apartment," I said softly and I saw Justin's eyes light up. "Live with me, Justin," I whispered against his lips. He grinned and kissed me, rolling me over so he was on top of me. He pulled away slowly, smiling.

"Of course I will," he whispered and I grinned and closed the gap between us again.

"I love you," I breathed.

"I love you," he replied, leaning his forehead against mine. I sighed in content, a smile on my lips.

Chapter 38

Almost a year later, Chris and I were officially moved into our new apartment. It was incredible. Not the apartment, which, in itself, was nice, but the whole idea that I was living with Chris. I just couldn't get my head around it. It was a dream come true.

We'd rented a place about halfway between London and Southampton, so that we were equal distance from my parents as well as Chris' dad. And it wasn't a long drive into London, only about half an hour, and an even shorter train journey. Chris had also looked around a bit and had managed to land an internship at a small newspaper in London. As it was interning, it wasn't a paid job, but it was definitely leading him somewhere, and I was so proud of him. I had decided to go back to school, go to university. I wasn't sure what I wanted to do with my life, but I took a course in Business Management at Southampton University, and I really loved it. I hoped that once I graduated, I would have decided on what I wanted to do in the future.

It was 3 months after we had moved into our place and I was watching television. "There," I heard Chris say from the kitchen. I smiled softly and got up to see what he was doing.

"There what?" I asked my best friend, my lover, as I wrapped my arms around him from behind.

"We are now, officially, moved in," he smiled and I smiled as I pressed my lips against his neck.

"Why's that? We moved in months ago," I told him and he nodded.

"Yeah, but I finally unpacked the final box," he said and I tensed slightly, knowing what had been in the last box. Chris, sensing my change, turned and looked at me. He didn't appear to be upset. In fact, he was smiling gently. He turned around again and pointed at a single shelf on the wall of the kitchen, just above the table. The only object on the shelf, in the centre, was a picture of him, when he was about 5, and his mum. I smiled softly and then returned my eyes to Chris. "Do you think she will be happy there?" he whispered. I saw tears gather in his eyes and I tightened my arms around him.

"Yeah," I whispered back. "The kitchen was her favourite place in the house. She will now be able to watch over you when you do the cooking..." He blinked back his tears and nodded.

"You're right," he said softly. He then glanced at me out of the corner of his eye and smirked. "Who said I'm doing the cooking?" he asked and I laughed.

"If you trust me to cook, then fair enough, but I know you're not that stupid," I said, grinning, and Chris grinned and pecked my lips.

"True," he agreed. I smiled and leant my head on top of his as I held him and we both gazed at the picture of him and his mum.

A few long, silent minutes passed and I looked down at Chris and saw he had tears trickling silently down his cheeks. "She'd be so proud of you, Chris," I whispered and he lowered his head as he tried to swallow back his tears.

"Really?" he whispered, his voice shaking slightly.

"Really, baby," I said, raising his head and making him look into my eyes.

"Chris, *I'm* proud of you. She's your mum; she would be 100 times more proud of you than I am." Chris smiled and then wrapped his arms around my waist and buried his head in my shoulder.

"I love you," he whispered. I just tightened my hold around him, unsure if he was talking to me or his mum.

We then moved into the living room and I pulled him down onto our new sofa. He smiled and cuddled into my side and I smiled, holding him tightly. I kissed his forehead tenderly and then we sat silently, watching television, but not really taking anything in. I don't know what Chris was thinking about, but I was thinking about an event that happened nearly *two years ago.* It was strange to think that it had been so long since I'd first told Chris I loved him. So much had happened since then; some good, some not so good. And I couldn't help but think about everything that was to come. I had a list of things I wanted to come true in the near future; a proposal, a wedding, a honeymoon, an adoption, parenthood... If so much had happened to us in just 2 years, I couldn't wait to see what happens in the rest of our lives...

-The End-